W9-AGG-001

THE COUNTRY I COME FROM

MILKWEED EDITIONS

THE COUNTRY
I COME FROM

BY

MAURA STANTON

THE COUNTRY I COME FROM

© 1988. Text by Maura Stanton
© 1988. Graphics by R.W. Scholes

All rights reserved.

Printed in the United States of America.
Published in 1988 by *MILKWEED EDITIONS*.
Post Office Box 3226
Minneapolis, Minnesota 55403
Books may be ordered from the above address.
ISBN 0-915943-33-6
Library of Congress Catalog Card Number: 88-42977

91   90   89   2   3   4

Publication of this book is made possible by grant support from the Literature
Program of the National Endowment for the Arts, the Dayton Hudson Foundation for Dayton's and Target Stores, and by support from the Jerome Foundation, the Arts Development Fund of United Arts, and by the First Bank System
Foundation's Small Arts Funding Program.

Acknowledgments

The stories in this collection appeared in the following places:

The Alaska Quarterly Review: "Adam's Curse"
Crazyhorse: "Oz"
The Michigan Quarterly Review: "Nijinsky"; "The Sea Fairies"
Pen Short Story Collection: "John McCormack"
Ploughshares: "The Palace"
Telescope: "Scotland" (Under the title "The Fountain House")

I would like to thank Indiana University for two Summer Faculty Fellowships
which enabled me to complete this collection.

In memory of my father
Joseph Patrick Stanton
1915–1988
Chicago—Minneapolis

May the road rise to meet you.
May the wind be always at your back.

The country I come from is called the Midwest
— BOB DYLAN

THE COUNTRY I COME FROM

The Sea Fairies/ 9

Oz/ 25

Scotland/ 37

The Palace/ 45

John McCormack/ 59

Adam's Curse/ 71

Nijinsky/ 91

THE
SEA FAIRIES

I remember how it rained that December. The temperature ho-
vered around forty, never dropping low enough at night to
freeze the drops into flakes. The yards were sodden; the yellow
grass was dead, but the thick and luxuriant blades had not yet
been crushed by a snowfall. There were Christmas trees in many
of the windows I passed on the bus home from school, but they
did not seem cheerful. I longed for snow.

That day, when I reached my own front porch, and was folding my umbrella, I saw that my mother was looking out at me
through the little window in the door.

She opened the door. "Just leave your umbrella out there for
now," she said. "There's an emergency at the Lundbergs' and they
need you to baby-sit."

"Oh, no," I said. My feet were wet and I longed for a cup of
tea. All I wanted to do was sit down in the living room and look
at the lights on the Christmas tree.

"They've called everyone. They need someone to spend the
night. I said you'd do it."

"What's wrong?" I shook the water off my jacket onto the little
braided rug just inside the door, and wiped my shoes. My glasses
steamed over. I couldn't see anything.

"Mrs. Lundberg was hurt in a car accident. She's been taken to
the hospital, and Mr. Lundberg's out of town. Her sister
called — she got your name from one of the neighbors. She can't
keep the girls herself because her own kids have chicken pox."

"Will Mrs. Lundberg be all right?"

I took off my glasses. My mother was toying with the top button on her blouse.

"Her sister didn't seem to know much. She's pretty upset. The hospital called her, and she picked up the girls at school. As soon as you get there, she's going to the hospital."

"Those poor little girls," I said. "Let me change my clothes. I'm soaked."

I threw my books down on the end of the couch and hurried to the bedroom. I had baby-sat for the Lundberg girls only once, when their regular babysitter was sick. The Lundbergs lived five blocks away in one of the big houses across from the lake. My mother had never met Mrs. Lundberg. I had felt strange babysitting for them, awkward and shy as I was introduced to their little girls and shown through their large rooms. Mrs. Lundberg had worn a grey suit and tiny gold earrings. I remembered Mr. Lundberg's high forehead and receding, dark blond hair. He was a musician and traveled. I had liked the three girls — I could only remember two of their names, Christine and Lucia. What was the little one called?

I pulled on my jeans and laced my tennis shoes. I could hear the rain falling harder again, so I stuck an extra pair of socks into my pocket. I put my nightgown and robe into a canvas bag, then went into the bathroom for my toothbrush. One of my sisters had come home from grade school and had put a Christmas record on the record player. I listened to "Deck the Halls" as I combed my hair. I could hear the sound of pots and pans and running water from the kitchen as my mother started supper.

I went into the living room. My jacket was damp all the way through to the lining. I grabbed my books. I knew it was going to be a long night, and on Fridays there was nothing I liked on television. My sister had turned on the tree lights and was lying on the floor, rearranging the chipped plaster figures in the manger. I stopped to admire the tree and took a deep breath. I couldn't smell pine this year, but the tree looked pretty. We'd bought the right amount of tinsel and had hung it strand by strand, instead of throwing it in clumps. The old, familiar glass ornaments glittered. I looked up at my favorite silver ball, on a bough just beneath the angel at the top. Then, shivering, I went out into the rain.

The drops pouring off my umbrella seemed murky rather than clear, but I guessed it was the effect of the dusk. I passed many brightly lighted windows. I saw a white Christmas tree with blue balls and a tall Christmas tree with tiny, blinking lights. When I reached Edgewater, the houses were set so far back from the sidewalk and surrounded by so much shrubbery, that I couldn't see in the windows very well. I looked out at the sodden park and the black lake beyond it. I fancied that if I tried to walk to the lake, I would sink down through the marshy grass before I reached it. The lake seemed to have overflowed or to have risen up from underneath the ground, for the park lawn was spotted with pools of standing water.

The Lundbergs lived in a tall brick house. The front windows were blocked by two high spruce trees. I opened the wrought-iron front gate and walked up the long, curving sidewalk. The spruce boughs caught the rain like plates, then poured it off all at once when it grew too heavy, so I had to be careful not to get soaked as I stood on the front step.

I had to bang the knocker twice. Then the door was opened abruptly by a woman with damp, blond hair who looked like Mrs. Lundberg.

"You're the baby-sitter? Thank God!"

She stood back while I shook out my umbrella and stepped inside the door. "Just leave that in the hall."

I leaned my half-shut umbrella against the inside wall. I was afraid to open it, for there was an oriental rug on the oak floor, and once again I was intimidated by the huge, open stairway.

"I'm Ellen Darrell," the blond woman said. She was clumsily pulling on her wet coat, which had been hanging on a brass coat rack. "I'm Mrs. Lundberg's sister."

"How is she?" I asked.

"Oh, God. I don't know. They wouldn't tell me much on the phone, but she's in serious condition. She was in the operating room. I've got to get there." I could hear a sob in her voice, which she was struggling to keep under control. Her hair was coming undone from her French roll.

"Do the girls know?" I asked.

She lowered her voice at once. "They're in the kitchen. I just told them she was in the hospital. I didn't tell them about the operating room. But they know I'm upset. Christine's been crying."

"Is Mr. Lundberg coming?"

"He's stuck in Vermont. He can't get a plane out until the morning." She finally got her top button through the hole. "I'll try to call you later. And I'll be back in the morning — or I'll send my husband. He's trying to find someone to stay with my kids. I've got two sick ones." She looked at my jacket. "Why don't you hang that on the radiator in the kitchen. Won't this rain ever stop? No wonder Karen had an accident."

I took off my dripping jacket while Mrs. Darrell pulled a man's black umbrella out of the umbrella stand. She opened it wide to test it, then snapped it shut. "I'm going. The girls know you're here — you've been here before, haven't you?" She continued when I nodded. "I'm sure there's plenty to eat. I told the girls to make themselves sandwiches, but I saw some eggs . . . try to cheer them up. That's the most important thing."

"All right," I said.

She squeezed her eyes shut for a moment. "I've got to get a grip on myself." She opened her eyes, which were blue and wet. I thought she looked younger but less pretty than Mrs. Lundberg. Her face was plumper.

"I'll cheer them up," I said.

She nodded. She went outside, raising her umbrella immediately. I pulled the door shut, then wiped off my glasses. The tall grandfather clock under the stairway ticked loudly in the silence.

I went into the living room. The heavy curtains were still open. The tall side windows must have faced the direction of the wind, for the rain was beating against them. I could see nothing in the dusk outside beyond the grey waves of water on the glass.

The high-ceilinged room smelled of wax and pine. I stopped to look up at the shadowy Christmas tree, a Norway pine with long, slender needles. It was covered with curious ornaments of different shapes. I reached out to stroke the cold wood of the grand piano, then opened the French doors to the dining room. There were silver candelabra on the glossy mahogany table. The glass and china in the highboys against the wall tinkled slightly, jarred by my footfall. I remembered how I had turned on the chandelier the last time I was here, delighted by its crystal teardrops. But for some reason I did not feel like turning on a light just yet. I wanted to see the girls first.

I blinked at the glare when I pushed open the kitchen door. All the heat and light in the house seemed to be gathered in that comfortable room with its bronze-colored appliances and shiny floor. The three girls were sitting around the maple table. The smallest one was spreading peanut butter onto a piece of bread. Christine, the oldest, was leaning over the table, her head in her arms. Lucia was drinking a glass of milk. She smiled at me. There was a white ring around her mouth.

"Hello," I said, feeling awkward. "You remember me?"

Lucia nodded. Christine lifted her head. Her eyes were red and swollen. She visibly swallowed her tears. "Mother's in the hospital," she said.

"I know," I said. "I'm sure she'll be all right." I spotted the radiator Mrs. Darrell had mentioned. "I think I'll lay my jacket over there to dry out. And change my socks. It's really raining, isn't it?"

The smallest girl was looking at me suspiciously. She was holding her slice of bread and peanut butter in one hand, and flinched away as I passed her to get to the radiator. I wished I could remember her name.

"Is this enough to eat? Can I fix you something for supper?" I asked as I pulled on my socks. I hoped my tennis shoes would dry by morning. I pressed my hands against the radiator to warm them up.

"I'm not hungry," Christine said.

"I am," said Lucia. "I want some pizza."

"Is there any?"

"In the freezer," said Lucia. She scooted her chair out, and ran across the kitchen. "I'll get it. You just have to put it in the oven. We're not supposed to turn the oven on by ourselves."

I took the pizza out of the box, read the directions, and looked at the complicated stove for a long time. I finally found the right dial.

"Can we watch television after supper?" Lucia asked.

"Sure," I said.

"You've got to practice, Lucia," Christine said in a tight voice. "Just because Mother's not here—"

Lucia looked down at the floor. She sighed heavily.

"Do you play the piano?" I asked her.

"She plays the flute," Christine said.

I looked at Christine. She sat erect in her chair. She wasn't crying now, but she was pale, and the skin beneath her eyes was faintly discolored. Her thin blond hair was pushed back behind her ears. She had large, dark blue eyes. I remembered that last year she had said she was eleven.

"Do you play something?" I asked.

"The violin," she said. "Like my father. Adele is learning the piano. I play the piano, too." She stood up, smoothing her plaid wool kilt. "I'm going to practice."

"You should eat something first."

The smell of pizza was growing strong in the kitchen. She wrinkled her nose. "I'm just not hungry," she said. "I'll get a sandwich later if I am."

She left the kitchen. I glanced at Adele, who had finished her peanut butter slice and was staring at me. She had curly light brown hair with red highlights in it. I thought she must be six or seven.

"Do you want some pizza, Adele?" I asked.

"Where's Mommy? I want Mommy."

"Mommy's in the hospital, Adele," Lucia said. "She'll be home in the morning."

Adele's face puckered for a moment. I thought she was going to cry, but just then a large orange cat came out from under the table. "Kitty," she called.

"You have a cat," I said. "I didn't know you had a cat."

"His name is Whiskers," Lucia said. "Here's the pizza cutter."

I took the pizza out of the oven. I could hear Christine tuning her violin through the closed door. She began to play as I cut the pizza into even wedges.

"That's beautiful," I said, stopping to listen.

"That's her Bach partita," Lucia said. "She's been working on that for a long time."

Lucia got out three plates. I put a piece of pizza in front of Adele, but she pushed it away. "I want to play Sea Fairies," she said.

"What's Sea Fairies?" I asked.

"A game we play," Lucia said. "It comes from a book, but Christine tells us stories that aren't in the book."

"I'll show you." Adele jumped down from her chair. She ran out of the kitchen with the cat jogging behind her. During the few moments that the door was open, I could hear Christine's music clearly. It made me shiver.

"That's so lovely," I whispered.

Lucia cocked her head. She had blond hair the color of Christine's, but it was cut short and curled around her ears. "It is lovely," she said. "She's playing it perfectly tonight. She hasn't begun over once."

"Would she mind if I went in there to listen?"

"Don't," said Lucia. "It would make her nervous."

I finished my pizza. Adele came running back with a book in her hand, and again, while the door was open, the violin filled the kitchen. The beautiful notes were muffled as soon as the door was shut.

Adele put the book in front of me. It was a heavy, old book with a tattered, rose-colored cover. I opened it to the ornate title page: *The Sea Fairies* by L. Frank Baum.

"He wrote *The Wizard of Oz*," I said.

"I know." Lucia stroked the worn cover of the book.

"What's it about," I asked. "How do you play Sea Fairies?"

"First of all," said Lucia, "the Sea Fairies are mermaids who live in a palace under the sea, the most beautiful palace in the world. It's made of pearl and coral and pink seashells."

"And glass," added Adele. "And diamonds."

"Yes," agreed Lucia. "Now in the book, Trot and Captain Bill go down to visit the Sea Fairies. Trot is just an ordinary girl, and Captain Bill has a wooden leg."

"How can they breathe under water?" I asked.

Lucia smiled. "The Sea Fairies turn them into mermaids, too. Only Captain Bill is a merman, I guess. Trot is a little scared, but she likes it. Oh, it's so wonderful down there." Lucia closed her eyes. "And the Sea Fairies are so beautiful."

"Is that all?" I asked.

Lucia opened her eyes. She looked a little scornful. "Of course not. There's danger, too. Zog is a hideous monster. He keeps trying to destroy the Sea Fairies. The squid work for him. They color the sea black to hide him when he travels."

"But how do you play the game?"

"We need Christine. We've used up all the stories in the book, so she has to tell us new ones. Then we pretend. We take turns being the Queen of the Sea Fairies, or her sister, the Princess. Then one of us is always Trot."

"What about Captain Bill?"

Lucia shrugged. "We don't need him. We pretend he's still up in the rowboat."

"I want to be a Sea Fairy this time," said Adele. "I don't want to be Trot."

Christine had finished her piece. I thought she might play something else, but in a moment she came back into the kitchen. Her mouth was trembling. "I need a drink of water," she said in a jerky voice.

She turned on the tap, and filled a glass.

"Adele wants to play Sea Fairies," Lucia said.

"All right." Christine took only a sip from her glass. "Let's go into the other room." She looked at me. "Will you play?"

"Sure," I said.

"I told her how we play," said Lucia. "Is she a Sea Fairy?"

Christine frowned. "No. She's Trot."

"Then I'm a Sea Fairy!" Adele laughed happily.

I put the pizza dishes in the sink, and we followed Christine into the living room. It was much colder in the rest of the house. I felt as if I had dived underneath the sea, leaving the sun on the surface as I swam down into the gloomy depths. Christine had turned on two end table lamps in the living room, and the light on her music stand was still burning, but the corners of the large room were still shadowy. I was going to suggest that we turn on the tree lights, when I noticed that this tree had only ornaments. There were no strings of colored lights and no tinsel. The ornaments were handmade, mostly wooden. I noticed a little carved rocking horse, painted shiny red, a goldfish with blue scales, and a tiny, unpainted wooden angel.

"You sit there," Christine said, pointing to a high-backed chair beside the fireplace. I obeyed her. I could feel the coldness of the heavy brocade cushion through my jeans. "Did Lucia tell you what Zog can do? Once he made the water boiling hot, and the Sea Fairies almost died. Once he turned the water into ice."

"How did they escape?"

Christine stood erect on the tiles before the fireplace. Adele and Lucia sat side by side on the couch, watching her.

"The Sea Fairies have an invisible magic ring around them. They made one for Trot, too. If you close your eyes, you can feel it on your skin."

I saw that Adele and Lucia had closed their eyes. I closed my eyes, too. I grew conscious of my skin in the cold room. I reached up to smooth my hair and felt a tiny snap of electricity.

"Tonight," Christine said in a hushed, trembling voice, "something terrible has happened."

I opened my eyes. Adele and Lucia, holding hands now, continued to keep their eyes tightly shut. Christine's eyes were shut. I felt uneasy. I couldn't look away from Christine. She swayed slightly as she stood talking in front of the brass andirons, her face as closed as a sleeper's.

"Zog has captured the Queen of the Sea Fairies. She's a prisoner in the dungeon of his terrible castle. The rest of the Sea Fairies are at home in the Palace. They don't know what to do. Zog has sent his squid to color the water black, black as ink. The Sea Fairies can hardly see each other in the black water."

"Oh," Lucia murmured. She did not open her eyes.

"Zog has learned how the Sea Fairies make their magic circle. He has a gold cup full of poison and if the Queen of the Sea Fairies drinks the poison, her magic circle will dissolve. Then he'll have her forever. The Sea Fairies have got to rescue her, but they don't know what to do."

"The Princess has a magic wand," said Lucia. There was a pleading note in her voice which startled me.

"She can't find her magic wand in the black water. No, this time Trot is going to have to save the Queen of the Sea Fairies."

Christine opened her eyes and looked directly at me. "We're the Sea Fairies. Lucia is the Princess, Adele and I are hand-maidens. What should we do, Trot?"

"This is where the game starts," whispered Lucia, shaking her-self and releasing Adele's hand.

"Tell us your plan, then lead us on a rescue mission," said Christine in a tight voice.

Adele stood up on the couch, bouncing on the cushions, wav-ing her arms toward the windows. "Look at the black water," she cried.

We all looked at the windows. No one had closed the curtains. The rain was changing to sleet, and was pinging against the glass. It was completely night now, and the lights in the room were reflected dimly in the glass, as if they were really burning some-where else, through miles of murkiness.

"Let's see," I began lamely. "I guess we've got to sneak into Zog's castle when he isn't looking."

"How will we find it?" asked Lucia. "The water's black."

"Well," I said. "The squid work for Zog, but the eels work for us. The electric eels, the ones that light up. They'll lead us there."

"Good," said Christine. She was watching me closely.

"Now let's swim there!" cried Adele. Again she began waving her arms. She jumped off the couch as if she were diving.

"Not yet," Lucia said. "Trot has to work out the plan. The cas-tle gate is locked."

"But there's a secret passage," I said. "It's hidden by seaweed. The goldfish know where it is."

"The goldfish are good fish," Lucia said. "They've helped us before."

"But they won't this time," said Christine gloomily. "Zog made a trap for them. He caught them all in a big net, and they're down in his dungeon."

"Oh," sighed Adele.

"But one escaped," I said. I pointed at the Christmas tree, remembering the ornament I had seen earlier. "That one escaped, and it swam here to tell us."

The phone rang at that moment. Even though it was in the kitchen, and the door was shut, the shrill bell went through all of us like a knife.

"I'll get it," cried Christine. "It's Aunt Ellen."

The two younger girls ran after her. By the time I reached the kitchen, Christine was talking on the white wall phone. The others were watching her eagerly.

"But when will she be home?" I heard her say. Then she sighed. She listened for a while.

"How is she?" whispered Lucia fiercely, pulling at Christine's arm.

Christine lowered the receiver. She looked pale, and was holding herself rigidly. "She's sleeping, Aunt Ellen says. She wants to talk to you." Christine handed me the receiver.

Mrs. Darrell began speaking. Her voice was far away and so full of grief that it must surely have contradicted any reassurance she had tried to give Christine. "Are the girls still there? Are they all right?"

"Yes," I said. "They're fine."

"I just told Christine that her mother was sleeping. That's all I want the girls to know right now." Mrs. Darrell paused. "But my husband and I are coming back, and I wanted you to know, because I'd asked you to stay the night. You see, my sister passed away about an hour ago."

"Oh!" I cried involuntarily.

"Please don't say anything. I know the girls are right there. We'll tell them when we get there. Just keep them distracted until then. We'll take over. And you'll be able to go home."

"All right," I said. I wanted to say how sorry I was, but the three girls were listening intently to my every word. Christine had fastened her eyes to my face, and I was afraid that she would be able to read the least twitch of my muscles.

"We'll see you in about fifteen minutes. Or maybe longer. Someone said the roads are getting slick. But please, please don't say anything to the girls—don't tell them we're coming. This is going to be very, very hard. The doctors have given us some sedatives for them, in case. . . . " She trailed off.

"Don't worry about anything," I said as firmly as I could. "I'll take care of them. Please don't worry."

"Goodbye, then," she whispered, and hung up.

"What did she tell you?" Christine asked quickly.

"She wants me to cheer you up, that's all," I said. I took a deep breath to steady myself. "She just doesn't want you to feel—" The word "sad" was on the tip of my tongue. "She doesn't want you to feel bored," I said.

Christine looked at me searchingly. "She talked to you for a long time."

"We have to finish our game," I said.

"Good," said Adele.

Christine turned away. "I'm tired," she said. "I don't feel well."

"Oh, Christine!" Adele pulled at her kilt.

Lucia looked at me, then at her sister's back. "Let's play, Christine. There's nothing else to do."

"I just don't—" Christine's voice was choked. She couldn't finish.

Lucia swallowed nervously. "Christine?" she called.

"We've got to talk to that goldfish," I said hastily. "Let's go back in the living room. Come on, Christine." I grabbed Adele's hand. "Come on, Lucia."

Lucia followed me, and Christine came after her reluctantly. I stopped in front of the Christmas tree and pointed up at the goldfish ornament.

"He's out of breath," I said. "It took him a long time to swim here, but now he'll show us where the secret passage is."

"He's too tired to swim back," Christine said in a hopeless voice. "He'll never make it."

"But look how small he is." I unhooked the ornament, and put it into the pocket of Adele's smock. "He can ride with Princess Adele."

Adele smiled in delight. "We're going to save the Queen! Let's swim, let's swim!"

"But here come the swordfish," said Christine. She came around beside me, and pointed toward the hallway. Her lower lip was trembling. "Zog has sent the swordfish. They'll cut us to pieces."

"But Princess Lucia has a magic whistle. When she blows it, all the whales floating up on the top of the water will come diving down. They'll frighten the swordfish away."

Lucia pursed her lips and whistled.

"You see," I said. "Here come the whales. The Queen of the Sea Fairies once pulled a harpoon out of the side of a whale, and now all the whales love her."

"But the whales are afraid of Zog," Christine said. "He blows darts into their sides and puts them to sleep. They can't go near his castle."

"We'll go alone. The goldfish will show us the secret passage in the seaweed."

"Oh," said Christine. She looked down at the rug. "We're trapped in the seaweed. We're trapped."

Lucia and Adele dropped to the floor. "We're trapped," cried Adele. "You're trapped, Trot. The seaweed is wrapped all around you."

I fell to the floor. Christine knelt down beside me.

"Zog has brought the cup of poison to the Queen." Christine covered her face with her hands. "She doesn't know it's poison. She's going to drink it. And there's nothing we can do. Nothing!"

"The clams will cut the seaweed," I said, speaking directly to Christine. "Their shells have sharp edges." Then I added in a triumphant voice, "And the Queen knows there's poison in the cup!"

Christine looked at me through her fingers. "Does she know?"

"Of course she knows. She's the Queen. She's smarter than everyone. Zog thinks she drank the poison, but a little starfish floated by just then, and he looked away." I pointed up at the star on the top of the Christmas tree. All three girls looked up at it. "There. The Queen just poured the poison into a vase."

"Now what will she do?" asked Lucia.

"Zog is coming toward her," whispered Christine. "He's going to wrap her in his cloak and take her away forever."

"But she still has her magic circle," I insisted. "Zog doesn't know that. He won't be able to touch her."

Christine stretched out one hand, as if to ward off something invisible.

"She's tricked Zog," I said. "Now the Sea Fairies are inside the castle. Trot is swimming ahead, and the Sea Fairies are behind her. They're going to find the Queen." I got to my feet. "She's just behind that iron door."

Christine, still on her knees, stared blankly in the direction I was pointing. "Who will open the door?"

"You open it, Christine."

Christine looked up at my face. I met her eyes and held them as long as I could. She sighed, then got slowly to her feet, and squeezed her lids shut. "I've opened the door. Now we're swimming into the dungeon. We're not afraid but Zog is afraid. He's afraid of mortals. If a mortal ever touches him, he'll turn to ink. When he sees Trot, he shrieks. He shoots up through the water. And now the Queen is waiting for the Sea Fairies. She's smiling. Her tail is covered with pearls, and all the goldfish in the dungeon have made a golden cloak for her, the most beautiful cloak in the world."

I felt my heart pounding. The color had come back into Christine's face. But then I heard the ominous sound of someone at the front door.

"What is it?" Christine touched my sleeve lightly. I couldn't look at her.

"It's Aunt Ellen!" cried Adele, running into the hall.

"Aunt Ellen?" Lucia said in a puzzled voice, following Adele.

Christine gasped. She took a step away from me. "She's dead!" she wailed. She ran into the hall.

I backed away. I backed away into the dining room. I heard Mrs. Darrell's voice, then a man's voice. I backed into the kitchen, letting the door fall shut behind me.

I put on my wet tennis shoes. It took me a long time to tie the laces, because my fingers were shaking. I was buttoning my jacket when Mrs. Darrell came into the kitchen.

"I want to thank you for coming over," she said in a quavering voice as she reached into her purse. She held out some bills.

"No, no, I don't want any money," I said. I clutched my books and hurried out the back door.

It was much colder, and a wind was blowing, sweeping away the clouds, and opening a space in the sky for a huge, white moon. I was startled by the brightness. Ordinary fir trees had been transformed into glass. The bare oaks and dying elms of the neighborhood were all sparkling. Their weighted limbs made a crackling and popping sound. I had trouble keeping my balance as I walked down the alley. Car windshields were sheeted with shiny ice. Garbage cans glittered in the moonlight. It was as if Zog had worked one of his spells under cover of the black water. He had frozen the kingdom of the Sea Fairies, and only Trot, the ordinary girl, was allowed to swim to the surface to resume her life as if nothing had happened.

OZ

The barometer dropped. The light dimmed to a funny yellow. Massive clouds shifted and reshifted above the city. Everyone knew it meant tornados.

It was after supper. I sat on the back step, my elbows propped on my knees. For a while the heavy trees did not move. Every leaf appeared to be weighted by the atmosphere. The birds sounded shrill, and the two cardinals who lived in the yard kept flying back and forth between the gutter and the neighbor's elm. The woodpecker, who so irritated my father, landed on the T.V. aerial, pecked at the metal pole, and sent a moaning vibration through the house.

My mother appeared at the screen door. "Do you want some coffee?"

"No, thanks," I said.

My mother came out onto the steps with her blue mug. I made room for her to sit down.

"Where is everybody?"

"The girls are sewing in the basement. The others are upstairs playing a game. I don't know where Pat disappeared to."

"I saw him go down the alley with his basketball," I said. I glanced covertly at my mother, who had not smiled for three days, ever since my brother Joe had flown off to basic training in Louisiana. He had been drafted. His birthday had been the third date drawn on the television lottery, and everyone knew that he was destined for Vietnam. It made me feel strange inside when I considered that Joe was a year younger than I was.

"I called Danny at work," my mother said. "We're out of sugar."

"I hope he gets home before it pours. Did he ride his bike?"

My mother nodded. "I closed all the windows."

"I hate this kind of weather," I said. "It makes knots in my stomach."

My mother sipped her coffee, looking up at the sky. A breeze had sprung up, lifting a strand of her dark brown hair, which had once been as light as mine. That was before her first pregnancy, I knew. I had marveled at the old photographs.

"Did Dad call?"

She nodded. "He's in Rapid City. He'll be back Friday."

Suddenly the siren blared from the schoolyard three blocks away. We both jumped.

"They've sighted one." My mother stood up to scan the moving sky. "We'd better all get to the basement."

"I'll go get Pat," I said.

I ran down the backyard sidewalk. The wind took me by surprise in the alley. The trees heaved above me, and dark green leaves spun through the air. Neighbors were hurriedly folding up their lawn furniture.

"Pat!" I shouted. My voice seemed to stream back over my shoulder.

I spotted him at the end of the alley, dribbling his basketball as he walked home. Big drops of rain began to fall. I ran back to the house and stood under the awning outside the door. Pat continued to move slowly, still dribbling his basketball which grew increasingly hard for him to control in the wind.

"Hurry!" I shouted. "What's the matter with you?" I looked up at the roiling, black sky, then down at the peonies, whose heavy, pink heads had been blown almost flat.

The basketball rolled out of Pat's reach, and he had to chase it. The rain plastered his hair to his scalp. When I saw that he had finally reached the yard, I darted inside and ran down the basement stairs. I could hear the shrill, excited voice of the disc jockey on the top forty station that my sisters liked to listen to while they sewed. I went into the big room that was paneled half-way up with knotty pine. It was part playroom, part store room, and recently my father had moved down his desk and some of his books.

"They've sighted two tornados," my mother said. "Out near Lake Minnetonka. One of them touched down."

I sat on the old, flowered couch next to my mother. The little kids, who had brought down a Chinese checkers game, had scattered the marbles across the floor and were chasing each other around and around the ping-pong table. One of my sisters was hemming a jumper in the corner. Another had spread out a paper dress pattern on one end of the ping-pong table and was cutting some brown corduroy with pinking shears.

One of the little kids, Sonia, started to sing. "London Bridge is falling down, falling down!" she shouted at the top of her voice. She ran faster and faster, passing her brother.

"Hush!" I said. "We're listening to the radio. This is important."

Sonia sang to herself. Her lips moved as she kept running. Finally she collapsed in a heap by the desk. The radio began to play an announcement from the National Weather Service, explaining where to take shelter.

"Are we in the right part of the basement?" my little brother asked. He hoisted himself up on the bar, where the Christmas ornaments were stored. "Which way is North?"

"This is the right part," I said.

I could hear hail beating at the windows. I looked at the distracted face of my mother and wondered if she was worrying about tornados or thinking about Joe in the army.

"Where's Pat?" my mother asked in a moment. "Didn't he come in?"

"He must be upstairs," I said. "I'll go see."

I ran up the basement stairs before my mother could get up. The kitchen was dark but lit by flashes of lightning. Pat was standing on the back steps, under the awning.

"Are you crazy?" I said. "They spotted some tornados. Get downstairs before you worry mother sick."

Pat shook his head. "I'm teaching myself not to be afraid," he said. "Just in case."

"In case what?"

He shrugged.

"Please don't talk about enlisting anymore," I said. "You're only sixteen. Mother is upset enough as it is about Joe."

Pat stared out at the rain, saying nothing.

I returned to the basement. "He's just at the top of the stairs," I said, to reassure my mother. "It's raining pretty hard." I sat down on the floor next to Sonia.

The disc jockey, whose voice was almost hysterical, began announcing more tornado sightings. There were unconfirmed rumors of a destroyed trailer court in North Minneapolis. Someone had called to report a tornado in St. Louis Park.

"Should we go to the work room?" asked one of my sisters. "Aren't you supposed to stand against an inner wall, or under a door frame?"

"I'll go," said Sonia. She took my hand. Her skin felt clammy.

"That's only if you don't have a basement," I said. "We're all right here."

The lights flickered. Pat came down the stairs at last. There were water drops on his face. "Danny just called," he said. "He's going to stay at the store until this is over."

"Good," my mother said. "I hoped he'd have sense enough."

Pat flung himself into our father's desk chair. "What's worse," he said to mother. "Tornados or buzz bombs?"

She glanced at him speculatively. She had been an army nurse in London during World War II. "As long as you heard the buzz bomb coming, you felt safe," she said. "When you couldn't hear it, that meant it was about to fall."

"Did one ever fall near you?"

"All around me. But the hospital was never hit, thank God."

"Were you afraid?" Pat asked, his eyes lowered.

"I got used to being afraid, I guess."

"But you weren't afraid in France, were you?" I asked. "At the chateau?"

"That was towards the end of the war."

"Tell us about it again," one of my sisters asked as she knotted her thread.

We had all seen pictures of the chateau with its mansard roof, turrets, gatehouse and formal gardens. I loved the picture of my mother standing in front of a lake on which three swans floated. There was another picture of my mother and her friend, Lucy, in their winter uniforms at the top of a long avenue of snow-covered topiary trees.

"It was huge," my mother said. "When our unit was first stationed there, we slept in bedrooms with enormous gilt ceilings and French windows opening onto balconies. Later, after the patients arrived, we nurses moved up to the old servants' quarters, but those rooms were large, too. It was funny," she said, half closing her eyes, her voice husky as she tried to remember. "We got water from a big canvas Lister bag which was kept at the top of the grand staircase. The Germans were supposed to have poisoned the well before they retreated."

"Was the staircase marble?" I asked.

My mother nodded.

"Did you get to know any of the patients?" asked Pat.

"Some of them. There were a couple of boys from New Jersey who used to kid me about my Southern accent. Then there was a little skinny fellow, who'd been shot in the chest but was almost recovered. He did card tricks for us. We called him Ginger because he had red hair. And later on I got to know a boy named Glenn from Morehead, Kentucky—not too far from where I grew up. We used to talk about home. He was in love—" she stopped, biting her lip.

"With you?" I asked awkwardly. Everyone was looking at her. Only Pat had swiveled the desk chair to face a bookcase and seemed to be reading the titles of the books. Sheets of water covered the basement windows. I imagined that I was in a boat.

"Not with me. With my friend from Boston, Lucy Baxter."

"Did she love him?" I blurted out. Then I felt embarrassed, and coughed to cover myself.

"She was wild about him." My mother took a deep breath, and I knew she was about to tell a story that she had never told us before. "She used to wheel Glenn down to the nurses' lounge when nobody was using it, and play records for him. We had an old wind-up Victrola, and the Red Cross had given us a lot of old records. Lucy and I used to dance together."

"Together?" asked one of my sisters, raising her eyebrows.

Mother laughed. "All the nurses danced with each other."

"What kind of dances?" I leaned forward.

"Oh, fox trots and tangos. But mostly waltzes. Our favorite records were *Begin the Beguine* and part of something by Tchaikovsky called *Serenade for Strings*. That was Lucy's favorite. But she could play the piano, too. I remember one night—it was past midnight—when I'd left my book in the lounge. I went downstairs in my bathrobe and when I got to the door, I heard her playing something that she called a barcarole. The door was partly open. Glenn had been wheeled up beside her at the grand piano, and she kept looking at him as she played. Her face was radiant. I was about to turn around and go back to bed when she heard me. 'Frances,' she called. 'Come here a minute.' I went in. She ran up and hugged me. 'Glenn and I are going to be married!' I congratulated both of them. They kept smiling and holding hands. I wanted to leave them alone, but Lucy insisted on playing the Tchaikovsky record. Glenn wasn't supposed to stand yet, so she made me dance with her all around the room. She was still in uniform, but I was in my long, maroon bathrobe. Glenn laughed and laughed. Lucy had a bottle of champagne in her room, and she ran up to fetch it. Glenn talked on and on about how he and Lucy would show up at his mother's door in Morehead and eat biscuits and chicken. Then Lucy was going to take him for a ride in a swan boat in Boston and buy him a lobster. Lucy came back with the champagne. We toasted. We vowed we'd all be friends forever."

"And did they get married?" I asked.

Mother frowned. She pushed a lock of hair back from her forehead. "Glenn recovered. He recovered too quickly. He was sent back to the front and died in one of the last battles of the war."

"How awful!" I swallowed. "It sounds like a movie."

Mother looked at me sharply. She seemed about to say something, but she only shook her head. I flushed, and realized that I had misunderstood her story.

"What did Lucy do?" I asked after a pause.

"We had both been transferred to other hospitals by then. I wrote to her from Paris when I heard about Glenn, but she never replied. I wrote to her in Boston, too."

"You never heard from her again?"

"Never. That was so many years ago. We were so close. We used to go for long walks together on our days off. We told each other everything." My mother's voice shook. "And then, it was as if she were dead. Blown away. As if I only dreamed her."

A loud clap of thunder made me gasp. The lights flickered again.

"I think there's a flashlight in the middle drawer of the desk," my mother said, and I was relieved at the firmness that had come back into her tone. "We'd better keep it ready."

Pat fumbled in the drawer.

My little brother began swinging his legs and kicking his heels against the bar. "I wish we had a T.V. down here," he said. "Who wants to play Crazy Eights?"

Nobody answered him, for the lights went out suddenly. Sonia gave a strangled scream. Pat, who had found the flashlight, turned it on and swung the beam around the basement. It was hardly necessary, for lightning flared almost continuously at the windows. From across the room I watched my mother, whose face kept flashing into view. I thought about Lucy Baxter. She and my mother had gone to Paris on a pass once and had eaten army rations while they rode around in a horse-drawn carriage. They had both taken French lessons from a charwoman in wooden clogs who worked at the chateau, and later they discovered that she spoke some kind of dialect. Nobody could understand a word of their French. My mother had always spoken of Lucy in great detail and with deep affection. And now here was the ending of the story, which my mother had always known, which changed and darkened all the scenes before, and was still capable, after all these years, of disturbing the even pitch of my mother's voice. She had always spared us this ending.

"I think they just said Lake Harriet!" one of my sisters cried nervously as a clap of thunder drowned out the radio. "Someone's sighted a tornado over Lake Harriet!"

"That's only two miles from here," my mother said.

In the silence that followed the thunder, we all listened to a report from a mobile news unit which had reached the trailer court in North Minneapolis. We heard descriptions of uprooted trees and twisted metal. Roofs had been ripped off some trailers, and others were overturned. The reporter began to interview a sobbing woman who could not find her husband.

"I'm afraid," Sonia said. She moved closer to me.

"What a horrible night," one of my sisters said in a tight voice.

"Get further back from the window," mother said to Pat. "I hope Danny's all right."

"The store has a basement," Pat said. He slid his chair to the center of the room.

"Oh, no," Sonia groaned. "The cat! Where's Fluffy?"

"She'll be fine," I said. "She can see in the dark."

"She's upstairs." Sonia's voice trembled and rose. "She was on my bed. She'll be blown away!"

"No, she won't."

"I've got to get her." Sonia struggled to her feet. "We can't let her die up there."

"Hush, Sonia," mother said. "Cats can take care of themselves."

"Not Fluffy."

"I'll get her," I said. "Go sit on the couch, Sonia. Stop crying, I'll get her."

Before mother could stop me, I ran up the basement stairs. The lightning flared rapidly and garishly at the kitchen windows. I felt as if I had stepped out onto the deck of a ship. Thunder rumbled continuously. The rain fell in such torrents that each time the lightning flashed, it looked like grey waves breaking against the house.

I ran through the dining room, into the hallway and up the stairs. My brothers slept in the big room upstairs, but there was no sign of the cat on their empty, unmade beds. The spread was smooth and neat on Joe's bed in the corner, and I remembered with a little shock that he was gone. I lifted the edge of the spread and looked underneath the bed, then ran into the girls' room. It still smelled of the bottle of Lily of the Valley cologne that one of my sisters had spilled last month. Tennis shoes and loafers were scattered across the floor, and blouses and shorts hung from doorknobs and bedposts. In a bright flash of lightning, I saw a hairbrush on the dresser, with a few strands of hair caught in the bristles, as if someone had just been brushing her hair a moment ago.

I shivered. Suddenly I felt lonely and far away from everyone.

"Here kitty, kitty, kitty," I called. I felt the rumpled covers on the top bunk and looked in the closet.

A huge clap of thunder made me jump. I ran downstairs, my heart pounding. I stood at the door of my parents' bedroom, and called the cat again. Then I got down on my hands and knees, and lifted the heavy, fringed chenille spread. I touched something cold which made me draw back my hand in fright. Then I realized that it was my father's leather slipper.

The wind had begun to blow fiercely. It howled along the side of the house, and I could hear it whipping the branches of the mock orange against a window in my own room. I ran down the hall. The lightning flashed. I saw the clipboard on which I was writing a story called "The Robber Bridegroom" still waiting on my bed, and I remembered the last sentence I had written before I had been called to set the table for supper: "The old woman felt the arteries straining in her chest."

I put my hand against my own chest. "Kitty, kitty," I called, but my voice was choked somewhere in the back of my throat. I had never heard wind this loud before, and I remembered the descriptions I had read of approaching tornados: they always sounded like speeding trains.

The wind sounded like that. I heard a large branch crack and fall.

"Oh, my God," I said out loud. "Oh, my God!"

It seemed an immense distance back to the basement. I would

have to pass too many windows. I got down on my hands and
knees and crawled to the bathroom. I heard a sound in the tub,
and when I pushed back the shower curtain, I discovered the cat.

I got into the tub, picked up the cat who was cowering in terror, and stood with my back pressed against the tile wall. The cat
struggled, but I kept her against my shoulder until she quieted.
During a flash of lightning I saw myself in the mirror across
from the tub, my mouth open, my hair fallen around my face.
The roar of the wind was so deafening that it seemed as if the
house had already been picked up off its foundations, and was
spinning through space.

The wind reached a whistling pitch, and then I heard a sharp,
explosive crack. Somewhere in the house glass fell and shattered.
I closed my eyes in terror. I held the cat so tightly that she cried
and jumped out of my arms.

After a while, I grew conscious of the sound of the rain. The
wind had died down a little. I stepped cautiously out of the tub
and went down the hall. I stopped in amazement at the door of
the dining room. The windows had been blown out and rain was
being swept in gusts across the room. The far away lightning
kept the sky continuously lit. Broken glass gleamed on the dining
room table and on the carpet.

I put my hand on the back of a chair to steady myself. The
dining room and beyond the living room, where the windows
were also blown out, was strewn with leaves and flowers. Twigs
and small branches covered the floor. Mock orange blossoms had
been ripped off the bushes outside, and white petals were mixed
in with shards of glass. A long runner from a climbing rose bush,
with a cluster of red roses still growing along it, hung from the
buffet.

I ran through the living room, stumbling over elm branches.
On the coffee table I saw a dead sparrow which must have been
hurled in and knocked senseless against the wall. I hurried past it.
The windows on the front porch, facing another direction, were
still intact. I looked out over my neighborhood. The street was
impassable. Trees and branches had fallen across it in both directions. Shingles had been lifted from the roof of the house across

the street. A big poplar had fallen across a parked car in a drive-
way, crushing the hood.

I felt dizzy, as if I had been spinning and spinning. This must
be like the future, I thought. Your past did not blow away. It
was you who blew away. You looked out the window and
everything was different.

I spun around. The living room smelled of mud and greenery.
I ran breathlessly toward the basement, telling myself that my
family was all down there, all of them, every one.

SCOTLAND

We were in the backyard when our new neighbor came over, wheeling her bicycle, dressed in her plaid uniform skirt, but without her class tie. Those of us not inside helping unpack were now sitting on the picnic table bench, and we ducked our heads and looked shyly at this stranger.

She jabbed at the kickstand. Smiling, still holding onto one of the handle bars as if she were afraid that the girl's blue bicycle would tip over after all, she said in a clear voice:

"I'm Susan. I live across the alley."

She was Margaret's older sister. Margaret had seen us drive up in the station wagon last night. She had stood on the curb, swinging her blue tie, asking us personal questions as we ran, delighted, in and out of our new house. Right away she had guessed we were Catholics. She had explained that her blue tie meant that she was a freshman at St. Dominic's high school, which would be letting out next week. Her sister Susan — we were to notice her yellow tie — was a sophomore.

Now Susan, standing beside her bicycle on slightly bent ankles, smiled at us. She was a thick, solid girl with short, tightly waved hair, and although she was not as pretty as Margaret, she looked dependable. She had shadows underneath her eyes, slight pouches which suggested that she studied past our own bedtimes, or that she needed glasses. Her legs, above pink knee-highs that matched one of the many colors in her plaid skirt, appeared startlingly white and the skin bulged at the elastic. She wore heavy cream-and-white saddle oxfords.

"Are any of you my age?" she asked.

We began telling our ages. She listened, leaning a little forward, so that her bra cups pushed out the front of her stiff and shiny uniform blouse; but we felt, as she glanced at each of our faces in turn, that we were all given equal attention. And although we knew that some day she would have to choose our oldest sister for a particular friend, we were grateful that she had not immediately designated her.

We all sat in a row on our bench, facing her. We were brothers and sisters in a strange city and it was too soon for any of us to have a friend. Our thin, bare arms touched as we shifted or gestured in our low replies or swatted at the mosquitoes that were beginning to flicker through the dusk. Susan's blouse grew white and luminescent. She kept talking at us, but it was hard to see her face.

"Hey, you kids!" said our father, invisible behind the screen door. "Get in here!"

"We have to go," one of us said politely to Susan.

She flicked up her kickstand with the toe of her shoe. "I'll come over tomorrow night. I'll take you to see the fountain house."

"The fountain house!" a few of us exclaimed.

"You'll see," she said, and there was something narrow and secretive about her mouth, so that even the boys did not ask her any more questions.

Susan called "good-bye" as we hurried inside one after the other. A mosquito whirred over our heads, and then we remembered that we had an upstairs window. An upstairs! Just like the children in the books about Scotland we were reading. We ran through the kitchen and the dining room to the stairway, and clattered up to the big attic room where the boys would sleep. We could see treetops from our window. We could see the roof of Susan and Margaret's house across the alley and a yellow light through the maple leaves.

We stood up there in the dark for a long time, looking out. Our arms kept brushing with little electric shocks. We hugged

ourselves. We could feel the fine, blond hair on our arms. We
had never been so happy or so certain that we were beginning
new lives.

* * * * *

We were wiping the dishes after supper. It was a pleasure to
put them away in the strange-smelling cabinets. We liked the
funny pattern in the linoleum. And there were two sinks, side by
side, with a faucet that slid between them. Last night we had
slept deeper and better than any time in our lives. In the morning
we had kept our eyes shut for as long as possible, pretending that
we were still in our old bedrooms, in order to prolong the surprise and wonder. Later, the boys kept finding excuses to run up
and down the stairs. The girls wandered from window to window, looking out at the lawn from different angles. In the afternoon, some of us had reread the best parts of the Scotland books,
those parts about the family's move from London, the new
house, the children's loneliness, and the part where the oldest boy
saves his sister's life on the moors. We had pestered our mother
for tea, and at last she had given us permission; we dropped the
tea bags carefully into the scoured pot and spread jelly on saltine
crackers.

Now, finishing the dishes, we discovered that the baby was
sleepy. Mother wanted to put the baby to bed, but we begged to
take him out in the stroller. We had all been invited to see the
fountain house. If one of us couldn't go, it wouldn't be fair.
Mother sat down in an old armchair, watching us button the baby's sweater. She played idly with the tortoise-shell glasses that
hung from a cord around her neck. Her face looked white and
tired.

We waited for Susan in the back yard. The younger ones
played "getting dizzy," spinning themselves around until the
house, the garage, the hedge and the maples blurred into a single
humming color. The older ones talked about the way the sky
seemed to stay whitish until past ten o'clock. We knew this was
true of Scotland, too, and the parallel made us shudder with hap-

piness. Still, we all watched the light anxiously. It was almost eight o'clock and not one of us had the courage to cross the alley and knock on Susan and Margaret's side door.

Finally Susan came. We heard the bang of a screen door, then the brisk pad of tennis shoes as she rounded the edge of the garage. She was wearing shorts, and her neck stood out from the cowl collar of her sleeveless top. Her hair, whose even waves were pinned behind her ears with gold butterfly clips, was fringed in a slight band over her forehead. The sharp tang of hairspray was not entirely masked by the sweetness of some dimestore cologne.

"Oh, the baby," she said. She knelt down and kissed the baby. "Let me push the stroller."

She put her hand on the metal bar. We were surprised at the pink sheen on her nails, which were pointed smoothly at the tips; yet her knuckles were hard and a little bluish. She pushed the stroller down the alley, and we all followed her or walked a little before her. We had only read about alleys in books, for we came from a subdivision in another state, where all the newly sodded lawns of the one-story houses ran into one another. We kept peering into the various back yards beyond the privet hedges, where we could see the flagstones of patios, or blue-black squares of grass. We liked the stucco garages and the shiny garbage cans in their neat wooden bins. In a few minutes the baby's fat chin fell down onto his little yellow bib, and his flat blue eyes closed. The coarse brown hair on his irregular skull lifted gently in the breeze caused by the motion of the stroller.

It was a charmed summer night. The faraway sunset threw a shimmering rosiness over the grey roofs of the houses, while a white moon floated in the east; a flock of starlings stirred and fluttered briefly up on the high telephone wire; the distant voices of children and the calls of mothers resounded through the screen windows giving onto the back yards, which were fragrant with purple roses, lily of the valley, rhubarb and spearmint; a cat walked in silhouette along the gutter of a garage, and under an occasional yellow porch light the air was already iridescent with tiny gnats.

We crossed the street and started down the alley of the next block. Then another alley branched off to the left, and we were passing the back yards of the bigger houses that fronted on the park. The second-story windows were brightly lit, although the shades were pulled; once the shadow of a man holding a book was seen frozen against the mysterious square.

A girl on a bicycle, pumping hard, rode past us. She had a gold locket around her neck that swung back and forth across her T-shirt. Susan stopped the stroller to look back at her.

"That's Amy Johnson," she said in a hushed voice, and we realized that she was giving us some special information. "That's Dan Johnson's little sister."

"Who's he?" one of the younger boys asked, but dashed off after a lightning bug without waiting for an answer.

"Oh, he's the handsomest —" she said, her voice murmurous as if she were talking down at the baby. "He's a senior."

Our oldest sister, the white calves of her legs flashing, suddenly ran down to the end of the alley and back again, her face flushed and her breathing noisy. One of the boys leapt up in the air, tossing an imaginary football over the moving stroller.

"I smell heather." Our oldest sister had paused a few yards ahead of the stroller, and was hugging her bare arms together. She looked thin and reedy, like the stalk of a flower that would go down in the next rainstorm.

"We smell it, too," some of us said.

"Heather!" Susan laughed. The stroller hit a bump at that moment and the baby woke up with a little cry. "I don't smell anything."

"We smell it."

Susan bent down and kissed the baby on the top of the head. He quieted.

"It smells like purple," our oldest sister said, her voice far away. She took deep breaths. "It grows on the moors."

"There aren't any moors around here. But there's a fountain," Susan said, raising her voice as the stroller wheels grated over some rough concrete. "We're almost there."

At the end of the alley, Susan turned the stroller onto the side-

walk, which dipped slightly downhill, so that an embankment of
neat grey stones, edged with moss, rose gradually on our left; we
could not see around the corner. Instinctively we let Susan and
the baby go first. The boys fell back, picking up pebbles or tracing greenish twigs along the cracks in the concrete, while some
of the girls patted the soft moss with their hands.

At the corner we paused, and a few of us gasped or sighed,
"Ah!" We stood bunched together, arms touching, looking at the
three arcs of golden water that fell from the central column of a
small fountain set into the yard of a brick house halfway down
the street. The color of the water changed rapidly, as we
watched, from gold to red to blue and then, astonishingly, the
three colors appeared together as each arc of the fountain was il-
luminated separately. Almost at the same time the shape of the
water changed; the central column magically diminished; several
thin ribbons of water rose from the edges of the basin and met in
the center while a fine spray of golden drops fell downward.

Susan had continued to push the baby up the street and was
standing as close to the fountain as possible without stepping off
the sidewalk. She looked back at us, and her dark, amused eyes
seemed to break the charm that had frozen us at the corner. We
ran to join her. Our oldest brother and sister lagged behind; they
were talking to each other and looking up at the sky where the
first stars had appeared, although it was still light outside. We
were worried that they would command us to go home; but then
our oldest brother lifted his arm and moved his index finger
against the sky, as if tracing a constellation, and there was such a
strange, dreamy expression on our oldest sister's face that our
alarm dropped.

"It's wonderful," we said to Susan. Our voices seemed to tremble
in the cooling air. We lifted the baby's head, and tried to make him
see, but he squirmed irritably, like a kitten held up to a mirror.

We watched the falling water until we could anticipate the
changes of color.

"Are they rich?" one of the boys asked loudly, pointing at the
neat but rather small house behind the fountain.

"It's the Ketchum's house," Susan said. She had stepped around toward the shadow of a blue spruce, where our oldest brother was now standing by himself. "Mr. Ketchum sells fountains."

"I wish we had a fountain," one of us said. The voice was disembodied in the dusk. Any one of us could have said it.

The baby whimpered. Our oldest sister picked him up and dandled him in her arms. She held him against her shoulder until his eyes closed again.

Abruptly the lights on the fountain went out. We gasped in surprise. We stood blinking, surrounded by blurry greyness. The pines and spruces rose up dark like the masts of ships, and the lights in nearby houses seemed brighter than before but further away.

"I'm cold," one of the girls said.

"Let's go," our oldest sister said. She carefully placed the baby back in the stroller, poking his little legs into position. She began to push the stroller. Under the first streetlight we saw that her face was sad and withdrawn, and we knew that something had changed in her and was changing in us. What could it be? Susan was walking behind us now, talking intimately to our oldest brother. Had she chosen him? But that was absurd. For we saw, by the way he kept his face averted from her and the stiff clenching and unclenching of his fists, that he did not want to be singled out. And in a moment he called sharply to the other boys, and they all began racing ahead of the rest of us down the alley.

Susan hurried to catch up with the stroller. She talked as lightly as before, but we sensed the slight annoyance in her voice. We looked at her critically. We knew what we would be saying later, that she wasn't pretty, that she was boy crazy, that she talked through her nose, that the hair on the nape of her neck had been cut funny, that her throat bobbed like a top when she swallowed. She was going to be our oldest sister's friend, and we couldn't stop it. Our poor oldest sister, who was too thin, too flat chested, too shy to ever have a date. Now she would start going around with this unattractive friend.

We were almost to our new house. The inner door was open, and a long rectangle of light streamed out into the unfamiliar blackness of the back yard. Through the still uncurtained windows, we saw our mother passing back and forth, performing some chore, her eyes downcast, her lips tight and unsmiling.

The boys ran inside at once, banging the door behind them.

"Let's go bike riding tomorrow night," Susan said breathlessly to our oldest sister. "You can borrow Margaret's bike. She's grounded."

"All right," our oldest sister said. Her voice was calm. She slapped at a mosquito that had landed on her arm. "I've got to go in. I'm getting eaten up." She turned to us. "You girls get inside with the baby. It's way past your bedtime."

We left her alone in the yard with Susan. In the kitchen we poured ourselves glasses of water from the cold water bottle in the refrigerator. It was hard to see past our own reflections in the glass, but when we looked out, five minutes later, we observed our oldest sister leaning on the picnic table, talking and laughing with Susan.

Later, when she came inside, we saw red bites on her arms.

"Was your new friend telling you secrets?" we asked, keeping our faces severe so that we wouldn't giggle.

"Maybe," she said.

"Does she have a boyfriend?"

"Who knows?"

"Maybe she'll find you a boyfriend."

Our oldest sister looked at the glasses sitting on the drain-board. "Wash those up before you go to bed," she said coldly. Her shoulder blades, which we could see through her light cotton blouse, appeared more angular than usual when she left the kitchen.

How badly we slept that night. We had to pass our oldest sister's bed to go to the bathroom, and we each in turn must have observed, in the glow from the hall light, how much she resembled us; and gazing alone into the medicine chest mirror at our own tender faces, we must have shivered at the return of our old pettiness and rivalry.

THE PALACE

After the wedding, I rode to the reception in a shiny black car. I sat in the back seat between two other bridesmaids. I was sixteen and light-headed with excitement. I had come up to Chicago on the train to be in my aunt's wedding. I wore a long satin dress, with an overskirt of yellow chiffon. The bodice was pinned in the back to make it fit in the bust. My high heels were of clear vinyl, through which I could see my toes, and I wore puckered nylon gloves which ran all the way to my elbows.

"What a beautiful ceremony," said the short bridesmaid on my left, whose name was Karen.

"Everything was so lovely," said the tall bridesmaid on my right, whose name I had never quite caught.

"That's the kind of wedding we all want." Karen sighed. She glanced at me. "Your orchid is crooked, sweetheart."

I adjusted the smooth petals on my shoulder. I had never seen an orchid before this afternoon, and I was surprised that it had no smell.

"Where did you say you were from?" the tall bridesmaid asked me in a voice that was sweeter and higher than normal. Because I was younger, and a stranger, the bridesmaids all talked to me differently than they talked to each other.

"Peoria," I said. "But we're moving to Minnesota this summer."

"Oh, how nice," said the tall bridesmaid.

"Isn't that the land of ten thousand lakes?" Karen laughed. "You know, I've never been north of Milwaukee."

"Did someone say Milwaukee?" The groomsman in a black tuxedo, who was driving, glanced back at us. "Best city in the country. That's where I'm from."

The two bridesmaids laughed, as if they thought he had told a joke. I leaned forward. It was a sunny March day. I could see the grey turrets of the Lakeshore Palace Hotel in the distance and high against the sky the red roofed cupola where I had always wanted to climb. I had been taken inside the hotel once by my grandparents when I was eight or nine, but all I could remember was drinking a limeade at the marble counter in the hotel's drug store.

"I'll park in the garage," the groomsman said. "I'll let you girls off at the front entrance."

"It's quicker to go in the back," said Karen.

"Oh, let's go in the front," said the tall bridesmaid. "I love walking through the lobby."

We drove under the green-striped canopy, and stopped at the bottom of a monumental staircase. Bellboys in red uniforms were running up and down the stairs. Our door was opened for us, and we stumbled out. The marble steps were slick under my high heels, and I held onto the brass railing. There were three sets of revolving doors at the top of the staircase, and I twirled through the one in the middle. I paused on the other side. I tilted my head back, looking up at the three tiers of balconies. The lobby was dim and bright at the same time. There were slender columns of rose-colored marble, oriental carpets, leather chairs arranged in intimate groupings, and crystal chandeliers. I had never seen anything so beautiful. I wanted to walk slowly around, touching the little cherry tables and the lion's head finials on the backs of antique chairs, but the other bridesmaids were moving swiftly toward the row of elevators. They entered one going down, and I almost lost my shoes as I hurried after them. The blond elevator boy closed the doors with a flourish. He pushed his buttons, then stood staring at the floor, whistling softly, never once looking at any of us.

The elevator door opened onto a long, brightly lit corridor. I was a little disappointed. The floor was only speckled gold tile and the ceiling low. We went into a large, windowless room where rows of tables with folding chairs had been set up for the wedding reception. My aunt and her new husband had already arrived and were posing for the photographer in front of an enormous cake, covered with silver roses. My aunt's lace veil had been thrown back from her face, and her cheeks were pink. Her dress was covered with little seed pearls which glittered under the bright lights.

"Oh, don't you look beautiful," my grandfather said when he caught sight of me. He put his arm around me. "Come take our picture," he called to one of my uncles, who had a camera around his neck. I smiled and blinked into the flash. My grandfather looked exceptionally handsome in his tuxedo; his pale grey hair was still thick and wavy. He had his picture taken with three of the other bridesmaids, and then with my grandmother, whose new pink suit could not hide her painfully hunched shoulders.

I stood at the very end of the reception line while the guests arrived. The room filled quickly. I met cousins I never knew I had, from Gary, Indiana, or visiting from Ireland. Sometimes they asked about my father or told me how pretty I looked in my bridesmaid dress. Two nuns in huge headdresses admired my little hat of yellow organdy petals. I nodded and smiled at everyone. Finally I shook hands with an old priest, who suddenly leaned forward and hugged me.

"I bet you don't remember me," he said jovially. "I'm your great uncle Pat."

"Oh, Father Pat," I said.

"I haven't seen you since you were twelve," he said, stepping back to look at me with his sharp blue eyes. He resembled my grandfather except that his skin was smooth and unwrinkled, and his voice had a more pronounced lilt to it.

"How are you?" I asked nervously.

"Fine, fine. And how's your pretty mother? I hear she's pregnant again."

"Yes," I said. "The baby's due any day now."

And how many will that make?"

"Nine," I said.

"And isn't your father here? Did he drive you up?"

I shook my head. "He had to work. I came up on the train by myself."

"Well, well," he said, moving away. "It won't be long before you'll be a bride yourself, will it?"

Finally the bridal party was able to sit down. Waiters in white jackets began pouring the champagne. I held my breath until they had filled my glass to the brim like everyone else's. I lifted it to my lips for the first toast, and it was as wonderful as I had expected. I drank the whole glass.

"Well, you're Irish all right," said Karen, who was sitting beside me at the end of the bridal party table.

"What do you mean?" I asked.

She pointed at my empty glass. Her own was still almost full. "I bet you're not even dizzy, are you?"

"No," I said. "I'd like some more."

She laughed. "So would the groom, but they're only letting him have one glass for the toast."

"Why only one?"

"Never mind," she said, putting a piece of wedding cake in her mouth.

I ate my chicken salad and had another glass of champagne. The musicians arrived, with their accordions, fiddles and flutes, and began to play something that sounded vaguely like the *Blue Danube Waltz*. The bride and the groom danced cheek to cheek while everyone applauded. Then they sat down and the Irish music began. Some of the guests clapped and others began singing "Who threw the overalls in Mrs. Murphy's chowder?" in gay voices. The waiters were still bringing champagne, but there were bottles of whiskey on some of the tables now, too. I saw Father Pat pour himself a shot.

"Do you think I could go walk around the hotel?" I asked Karen.

"Sure," she said. "They're going to push the tables back for dancing. We'll be here for hours."

I took the elevator back up to the lobby. Now I had time to notice the little shaded red lamps on the tables and the distinguished men in suits sitting here and there, reading newspapers. The front desk was a long, mahogany counter, with heavy, carved pillars, and I told myself that someday, when I grew up, I would check in here as a guest. I walked down a wide corridor, where gold lamps hung on the paneled walls, to the restaurant. I stood outside the French doors, half-hidden by potted palms, looking in at the glittering tables where I would sit some evening in the future. There were silver ice buckets or small silver coffee pots on all the tables, and the diners—there were not very many at this hour—brought their forks or wine glasses slowly to their mouths, as if they were doing so underwater. The women had bare arms like swimmers, and their hands moved in undulating gestures when they talked.

I went up a wide, thickly carpeted staircase to the first balcony. I heard exquisite music, and walked towards it. I came to some felt covered doors, one of which was propped open with a chair. A tall, gangly bellboy stood just outside, his face strained with attention. He seemed to be leaning in towards the music. I looked past him into the room. A string quartet was performing on a low platform in front of a small audience of men in tuxedos and women in evening gowns. I held my breath and listened. I had never heard music like this before. It was clear and ex-hilarating.

"What is it?" I whispered to the bellboy, who did not seem to hear me at first.

"Beethoven," he answered in a moment, speaking from the corner of his mouth. "It's the *Grosse Fugue*."

Just then a bald man in a white jacket got up from his chair and darted to the door. The bellboy backed away, coughing.

"Do you have a ticket, Miss?" the man asked me in a sharp voice.

"No," I said, stepping back with the bellboy. My face burned with embarrassment.

With one swift movement, the bald man removed the chair from the door and pulled it shut behind him. I could no longer hear the music.

"Dirty bastard!" The bellboy kicked the carpet as he walked away. His voice was choked.

I took a deep breath, then went up to the second balcony. I stopped to look at some large, dark paintings in heavy gilt frames. Some were portraits of dour-looking men, but others were huge historical canvases. It was hard to make them out in the dim light. I was left with an impression of twisted male torsos and chariot wheels. I had just paused to study the marble statue of a woman in a toga when I felt someone behind me.

I turned my head and caught a glimpse of a thin, jet-haired man in a rumpled sport shirt. His closeness made me uncomfortable, and I moved rapidly away. I went back down the two flights of stairs to the lobby, and decided to see if I could find my way up to the cupola.

I waited for an elevator, watching the numbers above the doors light up as the cars passed from floor to floor. When the first elevator going up arrived, I told the elevator boy the number of the top floor.

"I suppose you're going to a party in one of the penthouses," he said as he pulled the inner grate shut. "That's a real pretty dress." He smiled at me cheerfully. He had a bad complexion and a crew cut. His scalp showed in white patches above his ears.

"No," I said. "I'm at a wedding reception downstairs. But I want to go up that cupola. Do you know how to get there?"

"Sure. You're going to the right floor. There's a fire door in the middle of the hall. Just take the stairs. But watch out for the wind. Boy, is it windy up there!"

"Do you like working here?" I asked as the elevator jolted and rose. I pressed my hand against my stomach.

"It's great," the boy said. "You meet all kinds of people at the Palace. Celebrities, too. I rode with Cary Grant once. It's too bad they're tearing the place down."

"Tearing it down?"

"The land must be worth a million a square inch. They're going to put up apartments." The elevator stopped and he opened the door. "There you are. Maybe I'll catch you on the way down."

"Thanks," I said.

The fire door was right where he said it was. I could feel the wind in the stairwell, and as I climbed up the spiral stairs to the level of the open windows in the cupola, it made a whistling noise. At first, I could hardly open my eyes in the face of it. My hair was whipped back from my forehead. But then I grew used to its steady push against my body.

The lake was dazzling. No real sea could have pleased me better just then. The plane of the water seemed to tilt upwards towards a vaporous blue horizon, and across it ran foaming waves which broke on the rocks below me with stolid turbulence.

Then my eye caught the glint of the setting sun on the glass fronts of apartment buildings along Lake Shore Drive. I felt a pang. I would never see this view when I grew up—when the future came, this hotel would not exist. I ran my palm along the rough stone window ledge. It occurred to me for the first time that the other solid objects with which I had furnished my future would soon not exist—my home, my high school, and even my friends would all evaporate this summer when my family moved, and I could not begin to imagine what might replace them.

After a few minutes, I think I began to be self-conscious about my sadness. I told myself that I was grown up, that this was the way you felt as an adult. I threw my head back, and looked up at some soft hazy clouds that were gathering as the sun dropped. I tried to hum the scrap of Beethoven I had heard downstairs, but the melody eluded me. I could only faintly recall its effect on me.

I went slowly back down the spiral stairs, trying not to stumble in my wobbly heels. As I reached the fire door, I heard a grunt. In the corner of the stairwell stood the jet-haired man I had seen up on the second balcony. As I stared at him, startled and immediately uneasy, he fumbled with his pants and opened his fly.

"Here, Miss," he said softly, grinning at me.

I gasped, and ran past him. It took me a few moments to get the fire door open, for in my panic I kept pushing against it instead of pulling it open.

"You want it, don't you, Miss?" the man said, coming closer to me. "You'd like to put it in your mouth, wouldn't you, Miss?"

I pulled the door open at last. I ran down the hall towards the elevator. I saw one open and waiting and I knew I had to reach it before the doors closed, or I would be trapped. My right shoe came off, but just at that moment the elevator boy, who was not the same one who had brought me up, reached out to close the door.

"Wait!" I called, abandoning my shoe.

He held the door open for me. I hopped awkwardly into the elevator with one stockinged foot. Before I had time to catch my breath and ask him to wait until I got my shoe, he had put his elevator in motion. He had a sullen face and bitter, twisted lips, so I did not speak to him. I leaned back against the back wall, fighting tears and hysteria. "Be calm, be calm," I told myself over and over like a litany.

"Where to?" the elevator boy asked in a harsh voice.

"The basement," I said.

He shrugged and pushed a button.

We shot down so quickly that I felt sick to my stomach. When the door opened, I stepped out immediately. I found myself in a gloomy area with rough stone walls, and I realized that I was in a real basement that must be below the level of the reception room. I heard the elevator door shut behind me, and I knew at once that the elevator boy had been maliciously literal when he let me off down here. I decided to find a stairway up, rather than call him back.

I took off my other shoe. I walked between bins that were piled almost ceiling high with coal, and came to a huge furnace. The door of the furnace was open, and the flames shot up wildly. A man in overalls, covered with coal dust, was heaving coal inside with an iron shovel.

I was afraid to let him see me and hurried past him. I went up three wide steps into another part of the basement, which was noisy with the roar of washing machines. The floor was wet and soapy, for some of the machines were overflowing. Three black women in white cotton smocks were pulling sheets out of the large commercial dryers that lined one wall. The next room was loud with the clank of ironing machines. Here there were about a dozen exhausted-looking women, some black and some white, feeding sheets through the big rollers. The women were plastered with sweat, and their shoulders seemed permanently hunched. A few of them glanced up at me when I passed, but their faces remained blank and expressionless.

I found a stairway up at last. I had to stop in a rest room to take off my stockings and wash my feet, which were covered with soap and coal dust. I flinched when I looked at myself in the mirror. My eyes, staring back at me, seemed furtive, and there was an unpleasant thinness about my lips. I tried not to think about the jet-haired man, but his ugly image was imprinted on my brain as if I had deliberately taken a photograph.

I could hear the Irish music coming down the hall. It struck me as tinny and garish. The reception room was so hazy with cigarette smoke when I entered that I coughed and gasped. Everything in the room was blurry, and the smoke drifted in waves. My aunt was smoking in her satin gown, and her face looked grey and drawn. Her new husband was scratching under his collar. My uncle had drunk too much, and his embarrassing laugh rang through the room. I sat down beside Karen and noticed the sharp, envious expression on her face as she talked to my aunt. Across the room, the groom's sisters were whispering together in the corner, and I knew by the shape of their mouths that they were saying nasty things.

I looked around me in surprise. I seemed to have x-ray vision. The martyred expression on my grandmother's face was carefully studied. My grandfather, as he hopped about in his tuxedo, doing some kind of jig with a cousin from Ireland, was vain and self-centered. Everyone I looked at was pinched or mean or stunted in some way, and I knew I was no exception. I heard unkindness and jealousy in all the voices that rose around me in supposed merriment.

My aunt moved away. The back of her wedding gown, where she had been sitting, was all wrinkled. The tall bridesmaid came and sat down on the other side of Karen.

"I'm glad I'm not marrying into that family," she said in a low voice. "What a bitch his sister is."

"You'd think it was her wedding," Karen whispered back. "You know, she told me I ought to have gone on a diet. She said my dress was too tight."

"What a nerve!"

"Bitch."

I got up and went to sit beside Father Pat, who was staring at the empty shot glass in front of him.

"What happened to your shoes?" he asked. He spoke slowly, his words faintly slurred.

"My feet hurt," I said, flushing and looking away from him. I knew I would never tell anyone what had happened as long as I lived, but I would never be able to forget it.

"Somebody said you were upstairs."

"I was looking around the hotel."

"It's a grand place." He slid his empty glass back and forth along the tablecloth.

"They're going to tear it down," I said before I could stop myself. I knew I was speaking out of meanness.

"Are they now? I read something in the paper, but that was a long time ago. I thought it had blown over." He picked up the shot glass and looked at it curiously. "They tear everything down. By the time you're my age, everything you used to like will be gone."

I looked at the tablecloth, which was covered with bread crumbs and specks of frosting.

"When I went back to Ireland two summers ago," Father Pat continued, "they'd even torn down the church where I said my first Mass. De-consecrated the building and torn it down." He sighed. He reached across the table for the whiskey bottle and poured himself another shot.

I looked at his profile as he put the glass to his lips. His hair was thinning over his temples, and I could see bluish veins through his fine, pale skin. The veins ran deep into his brain, where all the evil things he had heard in confession over the years must still be lodged, fresh and sharp as a packet of straight pins. Inside everyone's head, just below their pretty or bored or wandering eyes, the strangest and most frightening pictures must be permanently etched; yet the real world around them shifted and changed and disappeared.

I wanted to get up and go away somewhere and hide my face, but there was nowhere to go.

"Excuse me. You lost your shoe, didn't you?"

I looked up to see the cheerful bellboy with the crew cut who had taken me up to the cupola. He held my high heel in one hand.

I found this in the hall," he said, blushing until his ears turned red. "I thought it must be yours, so I came down here on my break."

"Oh, thank you," I said, taking the shoe from him. I found it hard to smile. He took a step backwards.

"Well, Cinderella, don't just sit there," said Father Pat with a sudden laugh. "Give the boy some cake. He might be a prince indeed."

"Would you like some cake?" I asked.

He hesitated. "Well, sure."

I got up, and led him over to the cake. The top two tiers were gone, and big chunks of the bottom tier had already been eaten.

"Do you like frosting?"

"That's the best part," the boy said, playing nervously with one of his gold uniform buttons. "You know, I thought of Cinderella, too."

"I didn't," I said.

"Didn't you always want to be Cinderella?"

"I'd rather be the fairy godmother," I said, cutting him a large piece of cake with a silver rose on the top. "So I could change things."

"I'll just take this back with me," the boy said as I handed him the paper plate. "I've only got ten minutes."

"Thanks a lot," I said. "It was very nice of you to bring my shoe."

He swallowed. "Don't mention it," he said. He looked a little hurt, and glanced around the room. "It looks like a swell party.

I'll have to get married someday just for the fun of it. See you later."

"Good bye," I said. I wished I could have been warmer to him, but my throat ached. My heart was a lump of coal. I went back to join Father Pat, just as my grandfather stood up, waving his arms at the musicians.

"I've got a song to sing," my grandfather cried, his eyes shining. "Do you know 'The Lambs on the Green Hills'?"

"Sure we do," shouted the accordion player, putting down his beer and adjusting his keyboard.

Father Pat whispered in my ear. "He used to sing that when we were boys. We stood on the hill together, looking at the sea. We thought we could see as far as America. Your grandfather always had a fine voice."

My grandfather began to sing. His tenor voice was high and clear, transcending his age in a way that startled me. I leaned forward. I had heard him singing around the house, in the shower and in the car, but never formally like this. He held onto the lapels of his tuxedo, his eyes closed:

The lambs on the green hills stood gazing at me,
And many strawberries grew round the salt sea,
And many strawberries grew round the salt sea,
And many a ship sailed the ocean.

He opened his eyes a moment, and I saw they were wet. The song went on, telling the story of a bride and the man she had not married, who was going to die for love of her, and who wanted her to sprinkle his grave with flowers so sweet. I could tell that my grandfather really saw the strawberries and the salt sea, and every time the song returned to the refrain, I saw them, too. And for a moment I was up in the cupola again, with the wind on my face, looking at the lake, with no knowledge of the jet-haired man who lurked at the foot of the stairs.

Father Pat had shut his eyes, too. His lips trembled. When the song was over, he shook himself.

"It gives me the shivers," he said. "I'm over seventy, and I thought I was a boy."

I wiped my forehead, which was covered with cold sweat. I

looked around the room at the other wedding guests, who were clapping and whistling and stamping their feet, trying to get my grandfather to sing again, which he refused to do. I felt as if a fever had broken. My grandmother touched my grandfather's hand when he sat down beside her. The groom had his arm about my aunt's shoulder and was whispering something in her ear which made her smile and look at her ring. People were laughing and having second helpings of the big, ruined cake, and it seemed to me that I knew even less about everything than I ever had.

JOHN
McCORMACK

The day was cool and grey and smelled of approaching rain. We wore sweaters even though it was August. We would have stayed inside to watch television that morning, except that our visiting uncle from Chicago sat in the big chair in the living room, smoking and staring at nothing. We were a little afraid of him, although he was kindly and gave us quarters when we bought him bags of popcorn or bottles of Pepsi at the store. He always had a glass of Pepsi beside him on the floor. He was supposed to be leaving in a few days. He was a plasterer, and there were some unfinished jobs waiting for him back in Chicago. He had been up north taking the "cure" he told us. "Cure for what?" we asked. "Booze," he had answered in a low voice. "But don't tell your mother I told you so."

We made cocoa in the spaghetti pot and sat around the picnic table in the back yard with our hot mugs, reading the new mystery books we had checked out of the library yesterday. Our oldest sister sat on the step, copying recipes from a thick *International Cookbook*. She had been reading cookbooks for a month and had a whole notebook full of recipes with ingredients we had never heard of before.

"How does this sound?" she would ask, interrupting us. "Norwegian Baked Herring."

"Awful!"

"It's layers of herring and potatoes. I think it sounds good. I've never tasted herring. Or how about this? Rice and Spinach Armenian."

"You don't like spinach," we told her. "You know you don't."

"I might, if it were cooked like this. I'd leave out the garlic, though."

We returned to our books. It was pleasant to look up occasionally to watch one of the cats roll in the mint that grew under the garage window or to listen to the piano next door. But after awhile, when we began to get chilly, we went inside to refill our mugs and decided to read at the kitchen table.

Our brother Joe, who had been over at the archery range all morning, suddenly appeared at the screen door, panting. A misty rain had begun, but he stayed outside on the steps. There were droplets in his dark blond hair.

"Something's happened at the lake!"

"What?" we all asked at once. "On our side?"

"This side of the bridge," he said. "I don't know what it is. But there's lots of police cars. I'm going back."

He jumped down the steps. We heard his shoes pounding on the walk around the side of the house. Our oldest sister hastily dropped the dipper back into the cocoa, and turned off the burner.

"Let me get my sweater," she said.

"Hurry!" We edged into the dining room to wait for her, setting off a tinkle of glasses in the sideboard. Our uncle, his back to us, was standing over the record player in the living room, humming "tura-lura-lura" to himself. He was about to play our father's old Irish record again. We heard the click as he changed the speed to 78, and noted the shiny red bald spot on the back of his head. His hair always seemed greasy, the way it parted over the bald spot. Yet he took a shower every morning, and when he shaved, he left the bathroom door half open, so that we had all seen him patting his cheeks with blue after-shave lotion.

* * * * *

Two police cars had been driven across the grass to the edge of the lake. We saw that first. Then we saw the boat and the diver

in the wet suit who was putting the oars in the oarlocks. A small
crowd of people had gathered at a short distance from the black
cars, mostly children in shorts, but there were a couple of
mothers, too, and the old man who lived in the tiny, unpainted
house down at the end of our alley. The surface of the lake was
dark and absorbed the drops of light rain without ripples.

Joe waved at us as we hurried across the thick, wet grass.

"They're dragging the lake," he said anxiously when we
reached his side. "Somebody drowned."

"Who?"

"A woman." He pointed to one of the police cars. A man was
hunched in the back seat, his head turned away from us to look
out at the lake. "That's her husband."

"Was she swimming?"

Joe shook his head. "It's awful," he said. "She jumped from the
bridge."

"Jumped?"

We all turned to look at the concrete bridge which arched
across the lake at its narrow neck. We were at the smaller, shal-
lower end of the lake, but there were still "Danger" and "Deep
Water" signs posted on the bridge pilings. We noticed how some
of the cars crossing the bridge slowed down as they spotted the
police cars on the shore.

"Why would she jump?" our brother Pat asked in a puzzled
voice.

"To kill herself."

Pat stared at Joe, frowning. He ran his hand absently through
his short, almost white hair. "Why?"

"She was unhappy, I guess." Joe looked out at the cold lake.
"But I don't know how anyone could be that unhappy."

We watched the diver and one of the policemen row out toward the bridge. The diver attached his face mask and dropped
silently into the water. He had a breathing tube, but it was hard
to spot it on the dark surface. Occasionally his head emerged.
Twice he climbed back into the rowboat, and the policeman
poured something to drink from a thermos. The other policemen
paced up and down the shore, rubbing their chilled hands togeth-

er, sometimes listening to the static and strange bursts of talk on their radio, occasionally speaking in low voices to the man in the back seat, who would roll the window down and lean out.

We squatted down, trying to cover our bare legs with the tails of our sweaters. The light rain turned into a fine mist, and the bridge looked silvery and insubstantial. The trees in the little woods behind the archery range were obscured by fog. More mothers had arrived. Some had come to fetch their children, but had remained standing near other mothers, talking in subdued voices and glancing out at the boat. Our oldest sister had found a stump to sit on, a little away from the crowd. Joe plucked at his bowstring absently and in a while went to sit by himself under the willow tree.

"Let's go home," one of us said after an hour. "I'm hungry."

We stood up. Our legs were stiff from the damp. The grass had printed greenish lines into our knees.

"Pat!" we called.

He ignored us. He was staring intently out at the lake.

We started home without him, glancing back at the police cars once or twice. We planned to come back after lunch. On the other side of the park road, where the grass was smooth and cropped for baseball, we broke into a run. We were out of breath by the time we reached our yard. The inner door was open, and through the screen we could hear two voices singing "The Harp That Once Thro' Tara's Halls." One voice, sweet and far away, was spoiled by static and crackles. The other voice, loud but weak and interrupted by a hacking cough, was our uncle's. We stood outside by the blue spruce for a minute or two, listening in embarrassment.

Finally we entered the house. Our uncle did not even hear us at first. His head was tilted toward the ceiling, his eyes were closed, and his hand was wrapped around his throat as he sang, as if he were controlling the pitch by the pressure of his fingers.

The song came to an end. Our uncle opened his eyes during the short band of static that followed and saw us as we crossed the living room.

He blinked and cleared his throat. "He was the best," he said to us thickly. "This old record doesn't do him justice."

"John McCormack?" we asked politely.

"John McCormack," he repeated. "I heard him sing once. That was at the ballroom of the Lakeshore Palace Hotel. It was at a banquet. All the men were wearing tuxedos, and all the women had on strapless gowns—I was a waiter. I never told you I was a waiter, did I?"

"No," we said as we backed shyly away from him, trying not to be rude.

"When he started to sing, I forgot I was supposed to be filling the water goblets. I just stood there, my mouth open. I felt it all the way up my spine, up and down every bone, in my skull—"

"Felt what?" one of us asked.

"I felt like I was dying, but it was so sweet. . . . he had the voice of an angel, a voice like the harp of an angel. I hope it's like that when I die; I hope the angels will sing 'Ireland, Mother Ireland' as beautifully as John McCormack."

"Somebody died at the lake," we said.

The vague, dreamy look on his face disappeared. "I know. One of the neighbors knocked at the door." He stood up heavily. "I need a walk. I suppose you're all going back there after lunch?"

We nodded.

"I'll go with you," he said as he headed toward the bathroom. "Your mother's at the store with the baby."

He came into the kitchen a few minutes later, and absently placed the John McCormack album on the table where we were making our sandwiches. He poured another Pepsi into his smudged glass. We stared at the album as we chewed. A brown castle had been sketched against the turquoise background, next to a portrait of John McCormack, who looked very handsome and foreign. He reminded us of our father in the old photographs on the mantel where he was wearing his army uniform and had a thick wave in his hair.

* * * * *

We did not like to be seen in public with our uncle, who walked stiffly, as if his legs hurt, and sang or hummed out loud even when he was passing a stranger on the sidewalk. His baggy trousers, splattered with paint around his cuffs, seemed about to fall down around his ankles. His black dress shoes were unpolished and worn at the heels. The back of his shirt was creased. The skin under his eyes was thick and swollen, his nose and cheeks reddened by broken veins. He always had a vacant, faraway look in his light blue eyes.

We were ashamed of our reluctance to be seen with him, however, and had never spoken of it to each other. We stayed close to his side as we crossed the park to the lake, pointing out interesting features of the neighborhood — the bus wye, the sycamore which had been split by lightning, the red ring of paint around a diseased elm, the archery range where Joe practiced with his bow and arrow, even the grove of trees in the distance where a man had exposed himself to some third-grade boys.

The rain had let up completely and the sun was coming out. The crowd had grown; now it was mostly adults, all of them silent, standing shoulder to shoulder as we came toward the shore of the lake. We recognized Mrs. Wagner, who lived across the alley; she was still in her nurse's uniform, standing on tiptoes in her white, rubber-soled shoes, trying to see over the heads in front of her. An ambulance had been parked next to the police cars. As we joined the crowd, we saw two policemen come around the side of the ambulance with a bundle. The doors were opened, then slammed shut. The crowd began moving apart.

Our oldest sister saw us, and jumped off the stump which must have given her an excellent view of what had happened.

"They found her," she said flatly. She tried to smooth her damp hair, which was beginning to dry in frizzy peaks.

"What did she look like?"

"I couldn't look after all. I only looked after they had her in the boat, covered up." She shivered. "But I saw her foot when they carried her out on shore."

"Where's Pat?" our uncle asked.

"Over there." Our oldest sister pointed to some bushes. "I

think he's throwing up. I should have sent him home—" She frowned, thrusting her hands into the pockets of her shorts and turning away.

We looked out at the lake. The surface was scaled with silver now that the sun was out and a wind was rising. The ambulance and the police car with the husband in the back pulled silently away. The diver stood by the rowboat, smoking and talking to two policemen.

Pat came up beside us. There were deep circles under his eyes, and he was wheezing slightly.

"You better use your inhaler," our oldest sister said.

"I'm all right."

"What did you see?" we asked.

"Her hair was so long it was caught in the weeds. They had to cut her free." He swallowed. "She was stiff. Her blouse was muddy."

Our uncle crossed himself.

Pat watched him closely. "Can you do that?"

"What?"

"Pray for her?"

Our uncle blinked. "Of course you can pray for her. For her soul."

"Isn't her soul in hell?"

Our uncle glanced down at Pat, then gripped his shoulder. "Now who told you that? Only God knows about the soul."

Pat trembled. His lips were blue and bitten, and for the first time we realized that he had seen something that was going to haunt him—something that he could not describe to us in words. We did not know whether to be envious or relieved that we had not seen it, too. Our oldest sister's guarded face told us nothing.

"We need to light a candle for her soul," our uncle said, bending closer to Pat. "I lit a candle when John McCormack died. That was in 1945 before any of you were born. I'd been sent home from the war with a bullet in my thigh. That candle burned for weeks and when it was almost out, I lit two more from the same flame. I like to think that other candles were lit from my flame, for other souls, and that my flame is still burning somehow. . . . or burned until John McCormack got out of Purgatory, the good man."

He brushed his hand across Pat's face, as if he had seen a tear which we had missed. "What do you say? Shall we go up to church and light a candle for this poor drowned lady?"

"Our new church doesn't have candles," we said.

"What? It's a Catholic church. Of course it has candles."

"We've never seen any candles," we said emphatically. "We go to mass every Sunday."

"There are candles," our oldest sister said. "In the vestibule on the far side, near the pamphlet table. It's the side we never go in—and they're way back in the corner."

"Let's go," our uncle said. "You can light the candle, Pat."

Pat nodded, and we started off across the grass which smelled fresh and sharp as the sun dried the blades. Other people who had seen the drowned woman brought ashore were moving slowly across the park, too, or standing in small groups, talking quietly. As we passed one group of women, which included Mrs. Wagner in her white uniform, we looked secretly up at their faces, but their moving lips and eyelashes and slightly knitted foreheads did not tell us what we needed to know.

* * * * *

We climbed the hill to the church, pausing a few times to let our uncle catch his breath. His face grew red and congested. The exertion caused his hair to stick to his forehead in wet coils.

Our church was a modern building of yellow brick, with a squat bell tower and a curved facade. It was attached to the older, three-story grade school. A few cars were parked in the lot.

"They must be hearing confession," we told our uncle.

He looked up at the church. "What a pity. You don't have any stained glass windows."

"The windows are colored glass," we said. "When the sun shines it turns all blue inside."

We led him to the nearest door, and held it open for him.

"Did you ever see Sacred Heart in Chicago?" he asked in a low voice. "When you go to mass at dawn, the whole church is as bleak as the inside of a mountain. You can't see the ceiling it's so high. Then the sun comes up—it pours through the center window, the Sacred Heart window, and you've never seen red that red. It's the color of wine or rubies or real, wet blood—" he coughed, glancing suddenly at Pat. "There's a gold canopy over the altar, too, and the candlesticks are massive silver. But the candles you light yourself are at the side altars."

We were inside the vestibule, a low, square room where a few metal folding chairs had been stacked against the wall. Another door, which our oldest sister opened, led into the church itself.

"The candles are on the other side," she said.

We dipped our hands into the aluminum holy water font as we entered. The water was cool and soft as we splashed it on our foreheads. The church was dim, for the sun was not hitting the blue windows this time of day. When we reached the center aisle, we genuflected. A large, abstract sculpture hung above the altar instead of the usual crucifix, and although we had gotten used to seeing it, we always felt a little funny when we crossed ourselves. Only two people were in line at the confession box on the left. The red light on the box at the right had already been turned off.

The vestibule on the other side of the church was shadowy, for the venetian blinds were shut. The pamphlet table was empty except for a few out-of-date copies of "The Catholic Messenger." We looked curiously at the tiered metal rack in the corner. Each shelf contained little red glasses with white votive candles inside. A black box with a slot in the top was attached to the side of the rack.

"That's strange," our uncle said, fumbling with the change in his pocket. "None of them are lit." He handed a dime to Pat. "Put that in the box."

The dime made a hollow clink as Pat dropped it in the slot.

"Let's see if I've got any matches, now." Our uncle began going through his other pocket. He pulled out nail clippers, ticket stubs, the broken end of a pencil, crushed grains of popcorn, three finely wrinkled one-dollar bills, and finally produced a matchbook with softened edges.

He was lighting a match for Pat when the inner door of the church opened. Father North, one of the three parish priests, appeared before us in his long, black cassock. He had just come from hearing confessions, for the purple stole still hung around his neck. We felt our throats constrict. His face was stern as if he had been listening to terrible sins.

He looked at our little group and his face darkened.

"You're the new children in the parish, aren't you?" he asked briskly.

"Yes, Father," we whispered back.

"Who is this man?" he asked. "Are you children all right?"

We stared at him, not understanding.

His lip twitched impatiently. "Is this man bothering you?"

We looked at our uncle then, stunned and horrified at what Father North was suggesting. He stood there in front of Pat with a match burning down to his finger, his mouth open a little, a slightly dazed look on his face. The white lining of his pockets hung partly out.

"Please, Father," our oldest sister said in a voice that was high and shaky. "This is our uncle." And then, although we had never seen her touch anyone affectionately before, not even our father or mother, she put her arm around our uncle's shoulder.

"He's from Chicago," we said, all of us speaking at once for we saw that our uncle's face was beginning to redden in shame. "He's our favorite uncle. You should hear him sing. We've come up to light a candle."

"Fine," Father North said. "But I'd like to lock the doors. Confession is over."

"Do you lock the doors in this church, Father?" our uncle asked in a soft voice, his eyes on the floor.

"It's not safe to keep the doors open when no one is here—it's a sorry comment on the world, I'm afraid."

Our uncle nodded.

Our oldest sister moved away from him, then, dropping her arm self-consciously.

Our uncle handed the matchbook to Pat. "Be careful," he said hoarsely.

Pat lit a match above the long wick of a candle in the first tier. It caught immediately and made the dark red glass translucent. He made the sign of the cross and bowed his head. We watched him pray for the woman who had drowned herself.

Then we turned to go.

Father North cleared his throat. "I'd appreciate it if you'd blow the candle out before you leave."

"Blow it out?" Pat looked at our uncle in surprise.

Father North pointed to a small sign taped to the side of the candle rack.

"What grade will you be in, son?"

"Fourth," said Pat.

"Can you read the sign?"

Pat swallowed. " 'Please do not leave candles burning. Fire — ' " he hesitated.

" 'Hazard'," Father North finished emphatically.

Pat looked at the candle flame. "I just lit it," he said, his voice quivering. "It's for a dead soul."

"Let it burn for a while, Father," our uncle asked in a voice so humble that we squirmed with embarrassment. "In most churches . . . ." his voice trailed off inaudibly.

Father North pointed at Pat. "Please blow out your candle. What if the curtains caught on fire? I know you lit it for a soul. Very nice. But it's not the candle that counts, it's the prayer behind it."

"I always thought it was the candle, Father," our uncle said.

Father North shook his head. "It's only a pretty custom."

"But I've lit a lot of candles over the years," our uncle said, his voice trembling. "You mean my candles did no one any good?"

Father North hesitated. Then his somber face lit up with a smile, the first we had ever seen across his face. We could see the edges of his teeth. "If they did *you* good, that's fine. That's important, too."

"I thought I was helping the poor souls out of Purgatory."

A flicker of annoyance crossed Father North's face. "Only God decides about that." He tugged nervously at the stole hanging from his neck, and pulled a set of heavy keys from his pocket. He looked severely at Pat.

Pat bent over the flame. We all drew our breath in and held it down in our lungs a long time until our chests ached, as if we could keep the flame burning by not breathing. We wanted a miracle, and when Pat's weak mouthful of air caused the flame to brighten, instead of go out, we thought we had been granted our prayer.

"Blow harder," Father North said.

"He has asthma," our oldest sister said.

Pat closed his eyes, then spat at the candle. The flame disappeared with a hiss. We knew it was the sound of a soul slipping into darkness, a soul that might have lit her way to heaven by the light of Pat's candle. That was our fancy, at least, when we glanced into Pat's cold and vacant face as he brushed past us and ran out the door.

"Good-bye, Father," we said hastily, to cover Pat's violent departure and the gloom which had fallen over our uncle's face, sealing his lips.

"Tell your brother to come see me sometime when his heart isn't so hard," Father North said. "You seem like a nice family."

"Thank you, Father," we said.

We walked home beside our uncle. He did not hum or talk about John McCormack, and we were afraid to mention the singer now. Our uncle's ankles seemed to hurt, for he walked even more slowly and carefully than usual, and he stumbled in places where the sidewalk was uneven or badly cracked.

Later that night we got out the box of old black and white photographs to show our uncle, who seemed despondent. We showed him pictures of ourselves at every age, in high chairs, in teeter-totters, in strollers, in matching dresses, in funny bonnets. When he held the photographs up to the light to see them better, we saw his ghostly fingers shining through the paper upon which our smiling faces had been, as we thought, permanently fixed.

ADAM'S CURSE

I could see my house from across the park when I got off the bus. The moon lit up the blue spruce in the front yard. If the sidewalk hadn't been so icy, I would have started to run even though I was exhausted after a night of standing in one place.

My father was still up and waiting to hear about my new job when I came in the door. He had been out of town for several days.

"Well, it's really simple," I said, pulling off my gloves and unbuttoning my heavy coat. "I stand behind this table near the escalator."

"She doesn't work for Woolworth's," my mother explained. "She works for this man who owns the concession. She only sells those log cabins I was telling you about—and the incense cones to put in the chimneys."

"My boss runs the sausage counter, too." I sat down on the couch beside two of my sisters, Claudia and June, who were already in their pajamas. "I'm glad I don't have to sell sausage."

"Are you getting minimum wage?" My father looked at me intently. His face was pale and the skin beneath his eyes seemed bruised. He had driven all the way from Kansas City.

"Twenty cents more," I said. "But the job only lasts until Christmas, you see. People only buy these things for Christmas."

"How many did you sell tonight?"

"Only three." I could feel myself blushing. My father was a salesman who traveled all over the Midwest.

"I wish I had a job," Claudia muttered.

"I'm tired," I said. "I'm not used to standing so long."

"I'll put the tea kettle on," my mother said. "There's some ham left if you want a sandwich."

"Just some cookies. I'm not really hungry."

I followed my mother out into the kitchen. I sat on the wooden stool and rolled my knee socks down to my ankles. I squeezed my calf muscles. I had gone to work immediately after school let out.

"My legs used to bother me during the nurses' training," my mother said, glancing at me as she poured old water out of the tin kettle and refilled it at the tap. "Working on the wards was exhausting."

"Is that when your veins got bad?"

"That happened later when I was pregnant."

"I'm supposed to keep some incense burning all the time," I said.

"That's nice. I like the smell of pine." My mother turned up the gas and put tea bags into two cups.

The kitchen was warm and cheerful. I liked the sound of the kettle about to boil.

"I guess I won't be eating supper at home for a while," I said. I think I was talking to myself.

"Are you sure you don't want a sandwich?"

"I'm sure."

"Will you be able to get your homework done, do you think?" My mother poured water into the tea cups and brought them over to the table.

"During study hall." I dipped my tea bag up and down in the water. "I've never worked a cash register before."

"It's good experience," my mother said. "I guess."

"I need the money for college. I can't just baby-sit anymore."

"You won't have much time for yourself, though. You won't have much time to read."

"I can read on the bus," I said. "And on my break."

My mother finished her tea quickly. She pushed her chair back.

"I'm really tired. The baby cried all afternoon. Do you want me to call you at the usual time?"

"A little earlier. I almost missed my bus this morning."

I sat sipping my cold tea until everyone in the house had used the bathroom. I heard my brothers giggling upstairs. The baby whimpered, then quieted. The clock in the living room chimed eleven.

I brushed my hair back from my forehead and suddenly caught a whiff of pine. I had burned cone after cone of pine incense in the little metal chimney of the log cabin which was used as a sample to attract Woolworth shoppers.

I meant to buy one of the log cabins for my mother to put on the mantel as a Christmas decoration. I was tired of trying to explain to people what I sold. It sounded funny.

*   *   *   *   *

When the clock chimed four, I sat up in bed. I was not sure if I had been asleep yet or not. Magnified images of my new job had been flickering across my brain all night. I kept seeing the coat room with the muddy floor where Woolworth's had required me to check not only my coat and school blazer, but my purse as well. I had been given a huge metal pin with an engraved number on the hasp which I had fastened to the band of my skirt. Over and over in my mind I saw the cash register, and my hands curled as if I were ringing up practice sales. I kept hearing the ping of the cash drawer opening. Smoke wavered up from a burning cone of incense. I stacked and restacked the log cabins, which were hollow, with carved openings for doors and windows. Little splinters burned in the tips of my fingers.

As I listened to Claudia breathing quietly in the other bed, I couldn't keep away the thought that had been in the back of my mind all night: I was horrified by my new job.

I buried my face in my familiar quilt, which smelled faintly of dry heat from the radiator.

The next day, during study hall, I raised my hand and got permission to go to the lavatory. I stood in front of the porcelain

sinks and looked at my face in the mirror. I would go to college
next year. Then I would get a job and probably work for the rest
of my life. I hoped I wouldn't always be this tired. My head felt
so thick and numb that when I bent over a book, my ears buzzed
and the lines of print blurred together. I splashed water on my
face, dried my skin with a brown paper towel, and returned to
my desk. I opened *Pride and Prejudice* once more to the assigned
chapter.

On the crowded bus downtown, a girl in huge angora mittens
sat down beside me. I could feel the girl watching me. My
fingers tightened on my purse and I stared out the window at the
rows of apartment houses flashing past in the early twilight.

"You work at Woolworth's, don't you?"

I turned to look at the girl, who had a solid, pretty face and
perfect teeth when she smiled. She had taken off one of the mittens and was picking at the wool.

"Yes," I nodded. "I just started."

"I thought I saw you on the bus last night, too. I got off before
you." The girl lowered her voice and spoke directly into my ear.
"You sell those Christmas cabins, don't you? Well, I'd like to
have one. You get one for me tonight, and I'll get something for
you. Would you like a candle? Or birthday paper?"

"What?" My eyes met the girl's eyes and slid away.

"I've got glue in my department, too." The girl laughed quietly. "Construction paper, glitter, bows, ribbon, anything like
that—next week I might be put in housewares, but that's all I can
offer tonight." She took off her other mitten, and reached into
her pocket. She pulled out a ring with an elaborate setting and a
glittering blue stone. "Marcy got me this the other night," she
whispered. "Pretty, isn't it? I don't wear it in Woolworth's, of
course!" She winked. "Do you have a tight waistband? Dropping
things down your blouse is the easiest way, although Marcy hid
this in her hair. Now that's clever!"

I felt my stomach turn over. "No thank you," I managed to say.

The girl patted my knee. "You'll get over being nervous. Just
see what you can do. I'll pick out something nice for you, you'll
see. My name's Carla, by the way." She shifted in her seat, and

pointed through the crowd of standing passengers. "That's Marcy up there in the red coat."

I could see nothing but heavy winter coats, scarves and shopping bags. The bus stopped at every corner, and more and more women crowded along the aisles. Carla offered her outer seat to an old woman with her arm in a cast, and disappeared toward the back of the bus. I started to shiver, but I told myself to relax. I was not going to steal. If Carla tried to give me something tonight, I simply would not take it.

* * * * * *

I had noticed the boy who grilled sandwiches behind the lunch counter passing by my table several times, and I was not surprised when he stopped in front of me.

"You haven't sold too many, have you?" he grinned. His voice was deep but low. He had a thin, narrow body. His hair was black and luxuriant, making his head seem disproportionately large.

"I've sold five," I said.

"You should smile more." He leaned toward me. His breath smelled of pickles.

"I try to smile." I could barely move my lips.

The boy nodded. He picked up one of the log cabins and held it close to his eyes, looking through one of the little windows. "I always wanted to live in a log cabin."

I shifted my feet.

"Yes, I always did." The boy abruptly stuffed the log cabin into the large pocket of his white, catsup-stained smock. "Here. I'll give you another sale." He reached under the smock to his pants pocket and pulled out a worn wallet. Then he frowned. "Whoops! Don't ring it up yet. I guess I'll pay you later."

I took my fingers off the keys of the cash register which I was about to punch. I felt a little dizzy.

"Well, then, you'd better—" I began, forcing myself to look at the boy.

But he had backed away. "See you later," he called. He darted down the cosmetic aisle to my left.

An old woman appeared beside me, breathing heavily. She wore a black overcoat with a worn fur collar. Her cuffs were trimmed in fur.

"He didn't pay you, did he?" the old woman whispered. "I could see him through the aquarium over there."

"He said he would later," I said.

"I'll bet he doesn't." The old woman, who wore a red wool stocking cap pulled down over her ears, shook her head. Her small face was withered and brown. I thought of the apples at the bottom of the bushel basket which my mother had thrown away last month.

"Would you like one of these?" I pointed at the log cabin on top of the stack. A greasy tendril of smoke rose from the incense cone in the chimney.

"Oh, no," said the old woman. "I never buy anything here." She looked over her shoulder. "I used to work here. I used to sell handkerchiefs. I had a whole aisle of handkerchiefs. Now they only sell big white handkerchiefs for men, but these were women's handkerchiefs, so pretty I couldn't help buying them myself. You should have seen them! Some were embroidered. Others were trimmed with lace or had scalloped edges. I sold hankies for little girls to take to church, too—why look!"

The old woman pulled a handkerchief from her coat pocket and spread it across the table. The yellowed cotton cloth was printed with large lilacs and the edges were scalloped.

"It's pretty," I said.

"Too pretty to use," the old woman said, folding her handkerchief neatly. "Are you going to work here forever?"

"Only until Christmas," I said.

"I'll give you some advice." The old woman leaned across the stack of log cabins. "Don't spend any money here—don't spend a dime. That's how they get your salary back, you see—you work for nothing then, and you end up poor. That's what happened to me."

"I'm saving for college," I said.

"I only come in to look at the fish." The old woman pulled on a pair of red gloves with white snowflakes woven into the wool. "When you're feeling tired, there's nothing so restful as fish."

The old woman clumped away. I looked up at the clock. It was finally time for my break. I locked my cash register, put the key in my pocket, and headed for the back stairs. My legs felt so heavy I could hardly lift them. I went first to the women's lavatory, where I had noticed an old leather couch in the outer room, but the three tough-looking girls in front of the sinks, who were smoking and tapping ashes into the basins, made me uncomfortable. I went instead to the little employee lounge down the hall from the cloakroom. The door was open but the light was out. I reached in to fumble for the light switch, then became aware that a boy and a girl were in the room, locked in a tight embrace, kissing passionately. I heard the suck of their mouths and their grunting murmurs. Enough light fell in from the hallway to reveal the white smock of the boy who made sandwiches. The girl was in shadow.

I jumped back, hoping I had not been seen. I had to sit down somewhere. I felt weak and dizzy. I went back downstairs. I saw some empty red stools at the lunch counter, and before I was quite aware of what I was doing, I had ordered a bowl of chicken noodle soup and a Coke. The soup when it came was lukewarm. I drank the Coke, and when I paid my tab at the register, I realized that the old woman was right. I had just spent an hour's worth of my salary.

* * * * *

The next day I sat in the high school lunchroom, drinking tea and trying to memorize the diagram of the legislative branch in my political science textbook. A bolt of pain kept stabbing through my head and my throat felt swollen. Every time I passed from one classroom to another, I took a long gulp of water from the fountain outside the lavatory, but it didn't help. Now I took a bite of my cheese sandwich, then placed it back in the waxed paper.

"Aren't you hungry?" Bonnie, a tall, broad-shouldered girl who ate lunch with me only on the days when her best friend, Rita, was absent from school, pulled over a chair from another table.

"I've got a sore throat," I said, closing my textbook. "I just don't feel like eating."

"It's going around." Bonnie tossed her brown lunch bag on the table and sat down. "Rita's out with it."

"I can't get sick," I said. "I've just got a job."

"So I hear. You've got old Adam's curse, just like the rest of us."

"What?" I said.

"Work." Bonnie laughed. "Because of him we all have to labor and toil and sweat. It's in Genesis."

I sipped my tea, my hand around my throat. "Where do you work? A hospital, isn't it?"

"Nursing home. I change bed pans, that sort of thing. It's pretty disgusting." Bonnie reached into her bag and pulled out some little foil packages. "Here. Put some honey in your tea. It's good for your throat."

I took one of the packages and pulled the tab. I watched the honey ooze into my half-empty cup. "Where do you get this? You always have honey."

"At work. They have big cartons of it for the patients. I help myself."

I looked into Bonnie's thick, calm face. "They don't mind?"

"They don't know and they probably don't want to know. It's an awful job. Who else would they get when they pay hardly anything?"

I said nothing. I sipped my cold, sweet tea and thought about Carla. I had avoided her last night by rushing out of the store to catch an earlier bus, but I would not always be so lucky. I knew I would never steal anything—I knew myself well enough to be absolutely sure of that—but I felt queasy and nervous, as if some huge, smothering net hung over my head, and the slightest jostle might cause it to fall.

* * * * *

It was snowing when I left school. I crossed the street and caught the bus going north, wishing passionately that I could get on the southbound bus and go home. Then I felt angry at myself. Most of the girls at my high school had jobs after school. Bonnie worked in the nursing home. Andrea often talked about her nightmarish job at the dry cleaners. And Susan had a boss who was always pretending to reach across her for something, and brushing against her breasts. I wasn't special. I was just like everyone else, and it was time that I realized it.

The bus moved slowly. A thick grey slush covered the busier streets, and the sidewalks were already white. Once I noticed a woman sweeping the snow from her front steps with a broom, but the flakes were falling so steadily that the concrete had already begun to whiten behind her.

I hunched in my coat, shivering. The heater in the wall of the bus did not seem to be working very well, and ice was beginning to form inside the windows. I rubbed out a clear circle with my finger so that I could see who was getting on at each stop. The bus was passing through the bad neighborhood now, and I saw a line of men in overcoats standing outside the Christian Brothers' soup kitchen.

At the next stop, the bus partially emptied. A lot of other people were waiting in the snow, however, and I remembered that this was where the buses from St. Paul crossed the river. I peered through my circle. Carla stood in the middle of a group of women who wore scarves and carried Christmas shopping bags. She was bareheaded, and clutched a green transfer slip with her angora mitten.

I reached into my book bag for *Pride and Prejudice*. I opened it at random on my lap. I looked fixedly at the white space between two lines of blurry print.

In a moment Carla was sitting beside me. She smelled of wet wool and wet hair. She shook herself, and drops of water fell across my pages, puckering the thin paper.

"Sorry!" Carla said. "What are you reading?"

I turned the book over so that the title showed.

"Oh, that!" Carla laughed "That's one of my favorite books. I never finished it, though."

"It's for my English class," I said.

Carla patted her wet hair with her mittens. "I missed you last night."

I forced myself to speak calmly, although my pulse was racing. "I guess I caught another bus."

Carla leaned across my lap, as if she had dropped something. "You're afraid," she murmured. She straightened up again.

I shook my head slightly. I looked out the window, but the ice had closed over my circle. "It's cold in here," I said.

"Here's your present." Carla pressed something light and smooth into my hands. I looked down. It was a tube of clear plastic filled with silver glitter.

"I can't take this." The tube seemed to burn my fingers. I dropped it back into Carla's lap.

"It's yours," Carla said. "It's a present."

"I can't take it."

"Would you rather have gold? It comes in gold." Carla picked up the tube and shook the glitter. "It looks like snow, doesn't it? I thought you might like it." She tried to hand the tube back to me. "It's yours. No strings attached."

I looked at Carla and shook my head rapidly. "No, please, I don't want it."

Carla continued to hold out the tube of glitter. "I like you," she said. "I really do. I want you to have it."

"I can't take it. I'm sorry."

Carla lowered her eyes. "You think I stole it, don't you?" she whispered. "Well, I didn't have time to steal it. I *bought* it for you. I bought it with my own money."

"I'm sorry," I said again. "I still can't take it." I felt wretched. I knew Carla was lying. I wished I could get up and move to another seat and never talk to another person on a bus as long as I lived.

"Well, you're not very friendly, then." Carla slipped the tube of glitter into one of her angora mittens. Without another word she stood up and made her way to the back of the bus. A middle-aged woman in a suede jacket sat down immediately in the empty seat, sighing with relief.

* * * * *

All evening I shivered in front of my table of log cabins. The store was drafty, and I had forgotten to wear a sweater under my school blazer, which I had checked in the cloakroom because my boss had asked me not to wear it on the floor. The burning pine incense was beginning to make me sick, and there was nowhere I could stand where I did not get a gust of smoke in my face every few minutes. I rang up a few sales; then for an hour no one came near my table. Right after my break, I remembered that I was supposed to buy a log cabin for my mother. I had two crumpled dollar bills in my pocket, so I rang up a log cabin and a box of incense on my cash register, put them in a bag with the receipt, and hurried up to the cloakroom. A girl in a pink, fuzzy sweater studied the receipt and sealed the bag with red tape. I checked it with my other things, then went back downstairs. I had five minutes left. I cut through the store, carefully avoiding Carla's department, and stepped out the main door. I took a deep breath of cold air, trying to clear away the sick smell of smoke which filled my head. It was only snowing lightly now. Christmas carols floated out from the brightly lit doors of the big department store across the street, and I wished I worked over there. I could see the tip of the huge chandelier which hung from the high, gilded ceiling.

Near closing time, I looked up from lighting another cone of incense to see my boss, who wore a heavy camel hair overcoat with a yellow sheepskin collar, standing over me. I blew out my match.

"How many tonight?"

"I've sold eight," I said, my voice cracking. My boss was partially bald. His forehead was narrow, and his nose slightly misshapen. The whites of his brown eyes were the color of heavy cream.

"Your register was short last night," he said.

"What?" I flushed. "I thought it came out all right."

"You were twenty-eight cents short," he said, his voice louder than it needed to be. I saw a woman shopper in the next aisle glance back over her shoulder.

"I counted the money twice," I said.

"Well, I know you high school girls," he said, leaning so close to me that I could feel his breath on my cheek. "You're always in a hurry to get out of here at night. You've got boyfriends and drive-ins to go to, don't you? But just remember. Until you go out that door at nine o'clock, you're on my time, not yours. And if you're short again, it'll come out of your paycheck. Understand?"

I nodded. I felt as if I were going to choke.

"Eight," he said, pulling back from me. "We're doing better in the shopping centers this year." He looked critically at my table. "You'd better light two more cabins. We'll catch them coming from the side aisles, too."

I placed incense cones into the chimneys of the cabins that he pointed at. I had trouble striking a match. My hands were trembling. At last I got the cones lit. The tips glowed, and tiny puffs of smoke rose into the air.

"That's better. I want you to smile more, too."

"Yes," I said.

I watched him until he disappeared in the direction of the sausage counter. The next hour went by slowly. My bones seemed to ache deep inside. My eyes burned, but I did not know if it was from the cold I was coming down with, or from the smoke. I closed out my cash register at nine o'clock, then counted the money over and over. As far as I could determine, there was no discrepancy with the register tape.

The lights in the store were almost out when I finally went up to the office with my canvas money bag, and got my coat from the cloakroom. I had missed my bus, and had to stand on the corner for fifteen minutes waiting for the next one. I thought the snow had stopped, but a cold wind was stirring the drifts along the curb and it was hard to tell.

At last the bus came. It was almost empty, and I sat by myself near the back. The snowplows were out, and for a long time the bus moved slowly in the path behind one of them. Then the plow turned off, and the road ahead was already cleared.

"Good night," the bus driver called gruffly when I got off at the end of the line.

"Good night." I tried to smile back at him, but the wind blowing across the park had already caused my face to stiffen.

My house was dark except for the porch light. It took me a long time to find my key, for my hands were almost immobilized by the cold. When I stepped inside the warm darkness at last, I saw that the night light in the dining room had been left on for me. For a moment I thought I smelled gingerbread. Then I reached up to pull off my hat, and the sweet, sickening odor of pine incense drifted out of my hair.

I could hear Claudia breathing regularly in the bedroom. Instead of turning on the light, I lifted the shade by my bed a little so that the streetlight on the corner shone into my room. The window pane was rimed with ice. I undressed hurriedly, found my flannel nightgown in the closet, and climbed into bed. The sheets were stiff and cold. I ached all over. I had meant to take some aspirin, but I was too weary to get up again. I closed my eyes.

In the dream that I remembered so vividly the next morning, I stood shivering in the snow before the door of a log cabin. I knocked and knocked for a long time, but no one came. At last the door swung open. An old woman in a fur bonnet drew me inside, pointing to a stone stairway that led down into the earth. "It's the stairway to hell," the old woman whispered. "No one ever comes back up it again."

"I've got to go down," I said. "I'm so cold up here."

I started down the stairs even though the old woman pleaded with me to come back. At first each step was treacherous and icy. I kept stumbling over dogs, who would lift their black muzzles for a moment, and then go back to sleep. But it grew warmer the further I descended, and at last I unbuttoned my coat. The stairway twisted around some boulders, and then led through a series of tunnels. I could see nothing, and moved ahead by touch. Suddenly I saw a light and stepped through an archway.

I was in my own living room. I recognized the worn green couch and the maple coffee table with its one yellow *National Geographic* on top of a stack of *Better Homes and Gardens*. My father, wearing his blue pajamas and leather slippers, was reading "The Art of Salesmanship" in the easy chair. He did not look up when I called to him, and I realized that I was invisible. I went to the window and pulled open the drapes. Instead of snow the air was thick with falling flakes of fire; the front yard was covered with ash, and the blue spruce was black and sooty, except where a few cinders still glowed along the branches.

Then I woke up, exhausted and depressed.

* * * * *

By the following night, I had begun to realize that I had more than just a cold. My whole body ached and my skin felt sore to touch. I could hardly swallow. But it was only Thursday, and I knew I had to keep going until the weekend. Luckily I didn't have to work this Saturday. That meant I had two whole days to rest and recover before the next miserable week began. The word "miserable" made me shiver when it crossed my mind, and I tried to suppress it. I was ashamed of the way I felt about my new job.

A cold front had moved in from Canada, and smoke from the downtown chimneys had frozen into white plumes against the sky. In the short walk from the bus to Woolworth's, my face grew so numb that I could hardly move my mouth.

The hours went by slowly. I felt faint and far away—the noisy chatter in the store echoed in my ears as if down a long tunnel. I sold only a few log cabins, even though I kept three incense cones burning steadily. On my break, I took two aspirin and sat on a folding chair in the employee lounge with my eyes closed. The naked electric bulb seemed to burn through my lids. I was glad when my ten minutes were up, but as I went back to my table, I hesitated. Carla, her long blond hair pinned back with two tortoise shell barrettes, was standing before the log cabins. She had one in her hand.

I turned and walked over to the pet department. I watched some striped fish swimming through the windows of a coral castle. When I finally returned to my table, Carla was gone. It was impossible to tell if any log cabins were missing from the stack.

The cold seemed to have driven most of the shoppers home early, for no one came near my table for the rest of the night. At nine I closed out my register and went upstairs. I buttoned even the top button on my coat, and wrapped my scarf carefully around my throat, which felt as if it were stuffed with burning cotton.

Just as I neared the door by the lunch counter, which was the only exit employees were allowed to use, I became aware of a commotion. The uniformed guard who checked the red tape on employee packages was glaring down at a girl who sat sobbing near the glass pie display. The store detective sat on the stool beside her, talking in a low but growling voice. I would have averted my eyes from the ugly scene and walked on past if the girl hadn't suddenly turned and lifted her face. It was Carla. Her eyes were red and wet.

"That's her!" Carla pointed at me. "Just ask her. You'll see."

I paused awkwardly. "What is it," I said through my scarf.

The store detective, a thin man with a grey crew cut, looked at me coldly. "You ever see this?"

He reached behind him and held up a log cabin.

"I sell them," I said. I did not seem to have enough breath.

"She sold it to me," Carla said in a choked voice. "She just forgot to give me a receipt, and when I realized I didn't have one I just stuck it in my pocket, that's all."

"Is this true?" the store detective asked.

I looked at Carla, huddled between the two men. The uniformed guard had said nothing, but he kept one large, reddened hand on Carla's shoulder. The store detective tapped his little finger impatiently.

"I don't remember," I said. I was surprised at the sound of my small, rushed voice. "I had a lot of customers tonight, and I don't remember any one in particular."

"But you remember me, don't you?" Carla asked. She looked unblinkingly into my eyes.

"I don't remember," I said again. The words felt like burned crumbs in my mouth.

"It was about eight o'clock," Carla said. "I was asking you about that Jane Austen book you're always reading on the bus. Remember, I asked you about what's-her-name, the one with all the sisters at the ball?"

"Look, Miss," the detective broke in, "have you seen this girl before or not?"

"I've seen her," I said.

"Did she buy anything from you tonight?"

I looked anxiously toward the door, where a small group of employees stood watching the scene. Although their faces were wary and disturbed, I had no way of telling what they really thought or wanted me to do. Then I noticed the lunch counter boy zipping up his parka. He ducked away from my gaze and slipped out the door behind the others.

"I don't think she did," I said. Then, as I saw Carla wince, I added quickly: "But maybe she bought it from the woman who sells them during the day."

The detective grunted. Abruptly he pulled off one of Carla's mittens and dumped it upside down on the counter. A Christmas candle wrapped in cellophane rolled along the Formica. He reached for Carla's purse, then, and along with a beaded wallet and a blue nylon hairbrush, he pulled out several boxed pen and pencil sets, some tubes of glitter, and several spools of red ribbon.

"Oh, Carla—" I trailed off helplessly.

Carla took off her other angora mitten and dumped out some mascara and gleaming gold lipsticks. She wiped her eyes with the back of her hand. "Oh, Carla, what?" she said. She stood up, shaking off the guard's hand, and reached behind her as she faced me. "Here's your present!" she said bitterly. "I think you deserve it after all."

Carla swung out her fist. She had an open tube of glitter in her hand, and before I could move backwards the air was filled with shining specks. I felt a shower like fine sand against my face. Little sharp specks stuck to my skin and spilled on down my coat, sticking to the rough wool.

"Get out of here," the detective said to me as I wiped my face with a tissue. "You girls are all alike. You lie and steal from the day you're born."

* * * * *

The next morning my mother insisted on taking my temperature. I sat on the wooden stool in the kitchen holding the glass thermometer between my lips. When my mother announced that I had a temperature of one hundred and three degrees, I felt a shudder of relief. I had barely slept all night. Over and over I had reenacted the scene with Carla and the detective at Woolworth's. Even when I was not consciously thinking about what had happened, I felt as if something black and monstrous was inside my skull.

I took some aspirin and went back to bed. I buried my face in my pillow and fell into a half-sleep, full of undefined but threatening shapes and shadows. I dreamed that my boss was strangling me, and when I woke up, I was coughing.

My mother brought in a cup of tea with milk and sugar. "How do you feel, Sweetheart?"

"I can't get warm."

"Drink this." My mother handed me the cup. "I called your school and told them you were sick. I called Woolworth's, too, and they said they'd get the message to your boss."

The hot tea seemed to run all through my body. The thought that I was not going to work tonight became clear to me for the first time. I felt more cheerful. My mother left to dress the baby. I sipped the rest of the tea. When I finally curled up under the covers, I dropped at last into a deep and solid sleep.

My fever rose and fell all weekend. On Saturday morning I got up to watch cartoons with my sisters, but by evening I was still running a temperature of close to one hundred and two. I made a nest out of my bed. On the table near me I kept a bottle of cough medicine, a spoon, a box of cherry cough drops, a bottle of Aspir-gum, a box of tissues, some Vick's Vapo-Rub, and *Pride and Prejudice*, which I read a paragraph at a time because my eyes burned. My mother brought me cups of tea and hot lemonade. Claudia brought me raisin toast, which was the only thing I felt like eating. I kept the lamp on the dresser burning when I napped after supper. I liked to pull the covers up to my neck and listen to the sounds of the house through my closed door. I could hear dishes clinking at times or the vacuum cleaner running. The television droned just at a level where I could make out only the commercials. My brothers and sisters laughed and squabbled. I could hear them running up and down the stairs, answering the phone, playing with the baby. Once they made popcorn, and the smell drifted into my room. The thought of returning to work remained in my mind as an ugly, black lump, but I discovered that I could screen myself from the realization by adjusting my pillow or by taking a hot mouthful of tea. Occasionally, however, I was disturbed by the smell of pine, which seemed to have penetrated my skin.

I still had a fever on Monday. I stayed in bed all day, except for an hour when I sat on the couch to watch part of an old movie on television. It made me dizzy and sick to my stomach to sit up, so I went back to bed and fell asleep. The house was quiet. Everyone was in school except the baby, and my father was on the way to Denver.

My mother woke me up.

"I just had a phone call from your boss." My mother sat down across from me on Claudia's bed. "It makes me angry."

"What is it?" I propped myself up on one elbow.

"He says he's hiring someone else because I couldn't tell him when you'd be back to work."

I blinked. "You mean I'm fired."

"He didn't put it that way, but that's what he meant. I told him I thought he was being unfair—everyone has the right to stay home from work when they're sick." My mother smoothed

Claudia's spread with her fingers as she talked. "He said he'd send you your check in the mail."

"Well, it isn't fair." I shook my head to clear it. "Couldn't he find a temporary substitute? That's what Woolworth's does. Or anyplace."

"He says not. He says he's a small operation." My mother stood up, frowning and pulling at her hair. "I guess there's nothing we can do."

"I guess not," I said in a dull voice. I felt irritable and upset, but shortly after my mother left the room, I began to consider what losing my job actually meant. I did not have to go down to the place ever again! I did not have to be ordered about by an ugly man with a sheepskin collar. I did not have to stand in one place until my legs felt as if they were going to collapse. And I never had to go into that depressing cloakroom and hand my purse over to the sullen girl behind the counter.

I sat up in bed, flushed and trembling. I guessed my trembling heart meant more than joy at my temporary release from work. I had been infected, like everyone else, with incurable resentment.

NIJINSKY

I pushed open the red door of my new high school. I still thought of it as my new school, although I had been enrolled since September and now it was almost the end of November. The low, modern hall was brightly lit. I was late. The doors were already shut on the soundproofed classrooms, and I could hear the hum of the fluorescent tubes hidden behind the translucent glass squares of the ceiling. I stopped at my locker and slowly changed into my heavy uniform saddle oxfords. I had nothing to fear. I had merely to go to the office, explain that my bus had broken down, and take an approved tardy slip to my first hour teacher. My new school was so different from the old school I had transferred from after three years that sometimes I felt light and thin, as if I were a person in a dream. I half expected the hands of the other girls to slide right through my body, especially when I stepped into the bright, noisy cafeteria with its small tables for four and its huge, abstract mural, or watched one of the softly veiled sisters, her head thrown back, laughing with a group of girls in the lounge.

My old school had been celebrating its Centennial when my family moved to Minnesota. Its high, sooty walls, its dim hallways and enormous flights of stairs had made me dread waking up on school mornings. The sisters were bitter and grim-faced; they were always collecting money for charity. There were even placards on the candy bar machine down in the sour-smelling basement cafeteria, where we ate our bag lunches in silence at long green tables.

I liked to think that I had changed since starting my senior year at the new school. But I was still nervous. I remembered the pinched-lipped Latin teacher, who used to humiliate me at the blackboard, with great vividness. Even though I had so far, in this new school, been able to recite my Spanish dialogues by heart, my throat clenched painfully when I rose to speak. But the black, kindly eyebrows of Sister Rosa reassured me.

I felt cheerful as I entered the main office. Waxy plants in straw baskets hung from the ceiling. Some oddly shaped leather chairs were grouped around a chrome coffee table. The secretary, typing at her blond wood desk, nodded routinely when I muttered my excuse, and handed me a slip of paper to fill in. She was young, and her nails were polished a frosty rose. She buzzed the principal's office, and in a minute Sister Olga swished out in her black and white habit, her rosary clicking against the metal door frame.

Sister Olga had a freckled, moon-shaped face. She smiled, and glanced at my excuse when I handed it to her. Then she bent over the desk and signed it with a felt-tipped pen.

"You're a senior, aren't you?" she asked.

"Yes, Sister."

"The seniors are meeting in the Little Theater this morning — and every Friday at this hour from now on."

"Yes, Sister."

She handed me the tardy slip. "One of our older sisters, from the Mother House in Wisconsin, is visiting us for a few months. She'll be giving lectures on music."

"Yes, Sister." I folded the paper in my hand. "Thank you, Sister."

I felt dismayed as I walked back down the hall to the Little Theater. It was one thing to appear late in my small religion class, which met first hour, and was taught by a friendly, overweight sister who liked to interrupt her theology with personal stories about her girlhood in Kansas City. But it was quite another thing to open the door of the Little Theater, where the whole senior class was assembled, and face a stranger. Still, the

sisters who taught at this school were pleasant and modern in
their views. I expected that I could slip unnoticed into a back
row seat. A few months ago, in my old school, I could not have
done it. I would have hidden in the lavatory. But I felt I had
changed. I was much less timid now, and could even talk animat-
edly to the other girls in my classes—I was not always pretending to read in homeroom.

The back of the Little Theater was dim when I opened the
door. The aisle slanted steeply down past bolted rows of red and
yellow and blue chairs. I heard the rustle of the other girls cran-
ing around to see who I was. I kept my eyes lowered, but
managed to spot an empty seat down on the left. I moved toward it, trying to appear casual.

"Young lady? Young lady, stop right where you are!"

The voice calling up to me was so sharp and querulous that a
great wave of heat washed across my face. I was stunned. I could
hear the girls around me holding in their breath.

"What do you think you are doing?"

I looked in the direction of the voice. The stage lights fell in a
circle, illuminating a tall sister who stood at the podium, just below the rim of the stage itself. She wore the huge, old-fashioned
headdress which all the other sisters of this order had abandoned.

"I asked you a question, young lady!"

I felt betrayed. I held out my slip of paper and struggled for
words. "I have a tardy slip, please, Sister."

"You have what?"

"A tardy slip," I repeated.

"And do you think that excuses you?·I was talking, and you
interrupted me. You opened that door. I was talking about one
of the most beautiful pieces of music in the world, and you came
in late!" Her voice rose. She raised her right hand and shook her
index finger wildly in the air.

"Sister, I'm sorry." The skin around my lips began to tingle. I
had always expected this kind of attack in my old school, but I
suddenly realized how much I had lowered my guard in the last
few months. I felt faint with humiliation, but at the same time I

knew that the salty lump in my throat was caused as much by anger as by tears.

"Sit down!"

"Yes, Sister."

"And if you ever interrupt me again—if any of you girls ever interrupt me again when I'm talking about art and beauty—I will deal with you personally, after school."

I sat down as quickly as possible. The girl beside me, who had long, straight hair that she must have ironed carefully every morning, raised her pale eyebrows discreetly and shook her head in the direction of the podium. I felt immediately comforted. I reached up to wipe the sweat off my forehead, but the same girl leaned toward me warningly.

"Don't touch your face," she hissed.

"What?"

She was unable to answer, for the sister at the podium was staring in our direction. I dropped my hands to my lap.

"Now I want you girls to listen to this music with pure souls," the tall sister said, her voice lower and calmer. At first I thought her white face was fuzzy, but looking at her more closely, I realized that her skin was only heavily wrinkled—her face, in the frame of her pleated wimple, looked like a drawing by Picasso. She extended her arms on either side of her body. "I don't want you to have any erotic thoughts when you listen to this music. It's beautiful music. Nijinsky was sorry afterwards for the evil way he danced. He was a pure man, a good man, but sometimes he was tormented. He always asked for forgiveness. We were close friends. Perhaps I'll tell you more about him sometime. But now I want you to listen to this beautiful music by Debussy."

She turned to a record player with fold-out speakers on the edge of the stage behind her, and touched the switch very quickly, as if she were afraid of it. A record dropped to the turntable and in a minute the haunting notes filled the Little Theater. The sister kept her back to us, and watched the record spin around as attentively as if it were a whole orchestra of musicians.

I took advantage of the music: "Are we going to be tested on this?"

The girl next to me shrugged. She shifted in her chair so that her mouth was close to my ear. "Her name's Sister Ursula. She says if you touch your face, you'll touch anything."

"What do you mean, touch your face?"

"Sex." The girl stifled a giggle. "She means sex."

* * * * *

Next Friday, we seniors were reminded over the P.A. system that we were to assemble in the Little Theater for another music lecture. It had begun to snow outside, and I was reluctant to leave my desk by the window. I could have sat there watching the flakes all day.

Sister Ursula was waiting for us at the podium, her arms folded. She watched us file silently to our seats. The room was chilly and damp, as if the registers, which were beginning to blow dry heat from the ceiling, had only just now been turned on. I rubbed my cold hands together, then tried to stick them up the sleeves of my brown uniform jacket. I thought I could see the shadow of the snow on the skylight above my head.

For a long time Sister Ursula only stared at us—she seemed to be looking us over row by row and face by face. I heard embarrassed coughs and nervous stirrings all around me. I kept my eyes focused at a point above Sister Ursula's headdress, hoping she did not remember me from last week. I had deliberately changed the part in my hair this morning.

My friend, Andrea, who sat beside me, scrunched down in her chair. Behind her hand she whispered: "I wish she'd get started."

"Me, too."

"She's spooky, isn't she?"

I nodded. Sister Ursula reminded me of the sisters who had terrified me in my old school—the Latin teacher, of course, and Sister Mary St. David, who measured our skirt lengths and rummaged through our purses, and the principal, Sister Vincent de Paul, who had once pinched my arm for breaking line to get a drink of water. I felt annoyed that I should be confronted with a specter from my gloomy, depressing past just as I was feeling comfortable in this brighter and more modern world.

"What man," Sister Ursula asked in a loud voice, "is the greatest dancer in the world?"

We looked uneasily at each other. Finally a thin girl with blond, greasy bangs raised her hand.

Sister Ursula nodded at her. "Stand when you answer."

The girl stood up. "Nijinsky was the greatest dancer, Sister."

"What do you mean—was?" Sister Ursula gripped the podium with both hands. She began to rock it back and forth.

The girl swallowed. "I mean—I think he's dead."

"Dead!" Sister Ursula shouted. "Of course he's not dead. Where did you get such an idea?"

"I don't know," the girl whispered, her neck and face coloring brightly. "I thought I read it somewhere."

"Sit down. Don't you ever answer a question with misinformation."

The girl sat down. I realized that the muscles in my stomach were clenched as tightly as if I myself had been Sister Ursula's victim.

"Now Nijinsky, of course, loved Stravinsky's music. One day he tried to explain how the 'Firebird' reminded him of God—we were walking together in Paris. I remember it was raining, and his hair was soaked." Sister Ursula shook her head. "But he was so happy—he didn't notice. He looked like an angel. Later we went to mass together."

Sister Ursula went on to talk about bassoons and oboes and descending chords, gesturing with her claw-like hands. I knew nothing about music. I had never heard of Nijinsky or Stravinsky or the other people that Sister Ursula kept talking about. I looked up at the skylight, hoping that the snow was still falling. I had no boots with me, but if it continued to fall all day it would nevertheless be a pleasure to feel the cold lumps in the arch of my shoe as I walked through the drifts. I began to hum Christmas carols in my head. I think I almost fell asleep, for I was startled by the first notes of the strange music which Sister Ursula suddenly began to play. But she switched the record off abruptly

after a minute. She came a few steps up the center aisle and stood
looming over the red-haired girl who sat at the end of my row,
resting her chin on her hands.

"What are you doing?" she hissed.

The girl gasped. "Sister?"

"What are you doing with your hands?"

"Nothing, Sister."

"Nothing? What do you mean, nothing? Take your hands away
from your face, do you hear?"

"Sister, I wasn't doing—I was just leaning—" the girl's voice
shook. She pressed both her freckled hands against her chest.

"You don't understand yet, do you?" Sister Ursula softened her
voice. She let out a sigh. She looked around at the rest of us.
"Never touch your faces, girls. Never. It's a terrible habit. If you
touch your face, if you play with your bangs, rub your nose, if
you even rest your chin on your fist no matter how inno-
cently—someone watching you knows what it means."

We stared at her blankly and uneasily. Andrea was pinching
the hem of her plaid skirt convulsively between her thumb and
index finger, and the girl on the other side of me had splayed her
fingers rigidly across both knees.

* * * * *

The snow fell slowly but steadily for the rest of the day. Hour
to hour and class to class I watched it stick and finally thicken on
the brown grass. Then it began to cover the sidewalks, and during Art, my last class, I could hear the clank of the janitor's shovel around the corner of the building. I kept looking up from the
piece of wood I was sanding to check on the flakes: they kept
coming down in eddying but satisfactory gusts. The Art teacher,
a young sister with strong hands and a bad complexion, kept
breaking out into bits of song as she went from table to table
checking on our work. In my old school we had done nothing in
Art except drawing exercises and still lifes, but in this class we
were always working with power tools, pouring cement into

molds, folding paper, breaking colored glass with hammers and twisting copper wire into shapes.

"You can go ahead with your first coat of stain," Sister Melissa said, bending over my shoulders.

But by the time I got my newspapers spread, my brush cleaned, and waited my turn for the can, the bell had rung.

"Shall I wait until Monday?" I asked.

"It shouldn't take you more than ten minutes," Sister Melissa laughed. "Artists don't work by the hour, you know."

I spread the reddish stain rather hastily across my piece of wood. The other girls in the class were rolling up their newspapers and gathering their books. My strokes were uneven and a hair from the brush stuck to the wood. I picked it off with my finger and left an ugly streak. I brushed over the wood again, trying to keep my strokes smooth. But I was impatient to get out in the snow.

At last I finished staining the edges and propped my piece of wood against the wall to dry. I was all alone in the Art room. Even Sister Melissa had disappeared. I pressed the lid back onto the can of stain, but as I gathered up my newspapers I knocked over the plastic cup holding the camel's hair brushes, scattering them across the floor. I got down on my hands and knees.

"What are you doing!" a familiar voice shouted at me. "Get up at once!"

I looked back over my shoulder. Sister Ursula stood in the middle of the Art room, her hands on her hips. She seemed very tall from my position on the floor. Her brown eyes shone under her heavily drooping lids. Her skin had the texture of a boiled potato.

"I'm picking up these brushes, Sister," I said, trying to keep my voice steady.

"Get up! You look like a dog down on all fours like that — what a shameful way to use your body."

I got slowly to my feet.

"Clumsy," she said, watching me. "Why are you so clumsy? And what terrible posture."

I stood facing Sister Ursula, my face burning. The windows

behind her were steamed up now, and I couldn't tell whether it was snowing or not.

"Touch your toes!"

"What, Sister?"

I stared at her headdress, with its elaborate pleats. Up close the linen seemed yellow — or it may have been the light. All day the story about Nijinsky's madness and death had been passed from senior to senior, for the girl Sister Ursula had humiliated had looked him up in the encyclopedia.

"Why are you standing there? Touch your toes," she repeated. "And don't crook your knees."

I leaned over and let my arms dangle. I felt frightened and light-headed. The muscles behind my knees strained sharply.

"Go on!"

I straightened up. "I can't, Sister. I'm too stiff."

"Stiff! You're a child."

"I can't do it, Sister."

She must have caught the note of hysteria in my voice, for she cocked her head and moved back a step. Suddenly she leaned over and with heavy, panting breaths began to touch the floor with the palms of her hands. She did it over and over. I stood watching her in horror. Her veil flew up over her headdress so that I saw its stiff underpinning. Each time she rose up, her face was redder and more congested than before. Finally she stopped and leaned against the blue cinder block wall, gasping for air.

"Are you all right, Sister?"

"Of course," she sputtered. She rearranged the front panel of her habit. "Just remember — " she began.

"Yes, Sister?"

"Just remember — " She took one final, deep breath, then seemed to recover, although her face was still a deep pink. "Just remember that when you dance, when you walk, when you move even a finger — you are praising God."

"Yes, Sister."

"When Nijinsky danced, he danced for God." She lowered her voice almost to a whisper. "He used to come to my room and dance. That was before I took my vows, you understand?"

I nodded. My whole face felt numb. I wanted to run past her but my books and folders were on the radiator across the room, and I needed them to do my homework that weekend.

"Right before my boat sailed," Sister Ursula went on, "he came to see me at the hotel. He begged me not to leave. I had to throw myself on the ground in front of my crucifix—I couldn't bear to look at him. He wanted to dance for me one more time but I was afraid to watch—I had dedicated myself to God, you see, just as he had dedicated himself—" She broke off with a sigh. Then her eyes seemed to focus on me more sharply. "Why are you so fidgety?"

"I have to catch a bus," I said quickly.

She looked at me sternly. "Then go. And keep your hair clean—you should be ashamed to let it get so oily."

I gathered up my books, my eyes stinging with unshed tears. Sister Ursula's last remark—since I had washed my hair only yesterday—caused me to mutter and blink my eyes in anger all the way home on the bus. I hardly noticed the snow. I kept going over the scene in my head—refusing, in many bitter phrases, to touch my toes. I told her over and over that Nijinsky was dead.

* * * * *

On Saturday I went tobogganing with Andrea. The sky was a deep and perfect blue; the snow seemed whiter than any snow I remembered. The sharp, cold air filling my lungs as we sped down the hill in the park was exhilarating; but each time, as Andrea steered us away from Minnehaha Creek, and we slid to a halt under the spruce trees where the ground was bumpy, I felt depressed. I could not keep the thought of Sister Ursula out of my mind, no matter how I tried. I was especially perplexed by the contrast between my dark uneasiness and the cheerfulness of everything around me—the glowing faces, the red and blue knit scarves, the laughter, and the flying mist of snow which rose up from under the speeding toboggans.

My fingers moved stiffly inside my mittens by the time we began to pull the toboggan home. We took the short cut around

Lake Nokomis, kicking up smooth, untrodden snow. My toes felt swollen in my boots even though I was wearing two pairs of socks. Nothing remained of the sun but a cold pink glow in the west.

"Why are they letting her do this to us?" I asked Andrea.

"Are you talking about that crazy nun again?" Her voice was muffled in her scarf. "If you're afraid she'll recognize you next Friday, cut class."

"And what about the Friday after? Anyway," I said, looking out at the grey lake which was beginning to thicken and freeze around the edges. "It's not just me. It's all of us. Do we have to sit there and be humiliated? Do we have to put up with all her weird ideas—next she'll tell us that Lincoln is still alive!"

"Ignore her, then." Andrea pointed to a shed which two men in red earmuffs were hammering together on the shore of the lake opposite the bridge. "Look! They're putting up the warming house—we'll be able to skate pretty soon."

"That's right where the woman drowned last summer, isn't it?"

"You have a morbid mind," Andrea said, jerking the rope on the toboggan so that it bumped across the sidewalk which circled the lake.

A wind was blowing across the snow. Andrea's words depressed me even more. I had been part of the crowd which watched the divers dredge the lake. I had seen the woman—who had committed suicide—brought up, and although she was wrapped immediately in plastic, I had glimpsed her heel, shriveled and grey as my own when I stayed too long in the bathtub.

* * * * *

I decided to speak to the principal about Sister Ursula Monday morning. I knew it was partly cowardice—I wanted to cover myself in the event that Sister Ursula singled me out again—but it was also partly benevolence, I told myself. The other seniors had never experienced these erratic and unpredictable outbursts from a teacher. There was no reason they should have to put up with the ugly and terrifying behavior that had finally given me—in Andrea's words—"a morbid mind." It also occurred to me that the other sisters on the staff had no way of knowing what was going on in the Little Theater on Friday mornings.

I was given an appointment to see Sister Olga during my afternoon study hour. I was tormented by the delay, for I knew from experience that my power to act diminished with reflection. I imagined the cold stare that would replace Sister Olga's friendly glance when I dared to criticize another sister. She would hate me for the rest of the year.

I could hardly swallow my bologna sandwich in the cafeteria. I sat by myself at a table by the window. The temperature had risen, and the dead grass was beginning to show in patches through the melting snow, which was by now heavily trodden and grey. I tried to invent another reason for wanting to see Sister Olga, but only half-heartedly. I knew I was doomed to go through with my idea. I had been deformed by the sisters at my old school—there was no other way of viewing it. I knew I hadn't been born with this morbid and gloomy vision. But years of submission to ridiculous whims had turned me into an unsmiling outcast—I looked at the groups of relaxed and normal girls at the tables around me with envy and despair.

At two o'clock I presented myself to the secretary. My face was already flaming with embarrassment, and my mouth felt dry. I was told to go into Sister Olga's office. She sat in a swivel chair behind her large, uncluttered desk. A metal crucifix with a burnished silver Christ hung behind her on the yellow cinder block wall. The wall behind the canvas Captain's chair, where Sister Olga gestured for me to sit, was covered with a huge pastel painting of indeterminate shapes—clouds or flower petals or waves.

"You're new this year, aren't you?" Sister Olga said. She nodded at me encouragingly. "What can I do for you?"

I swallowed. "I want to talk about—" My voice cracked. My lips felt so numb I could hardly move them.

Sister Olga stopped smiling. She leaned forward across her desk. Her eyes were intensely blue. "Don't be nervous," she said. "Anything you say to me will be held in the strictest confidence."

"Yes, Sister," I said.

"Are you having trouble with one of your classes, is that it?"

"No, Sister—not exactly, Sister. It's about Sister Ursula," I blurted out.

"Ah!" She blinked. She leaned back in her chair, folding her arms. "Go on. I think I know what you're going to say."

"She says if we touch our faces, it means we're evil—we're thinking about sex. She frightens people—she yells at us for no reason." I felt my voice warming, for the expression on Sister Olga's face was one of concern, not anger. "She thinks that Nijinsky—he was a famous ballet dancer—is still alive. But he died in 1950. She says she used to know him."

Sister Olga sighed. "Let me explain to you about Sister Ursula. I'd rather you didn't repeat this to any of the other girls, but since you've come to see me, I think it's only fair that I explain." She looked at me shrewdly. "You think Sister Ursula's crazy, don't you—because she thinks Nijinsky is alive?"

"I don't know, Sister," I murmured.

She shook her head. Her heavy nylon veil rustled against her round collar. "A very small part of our order has always been cloistered, you see. But we've agreed—in consultation with the Bishop—that the cloister is not a valid response to the modern world. Anyway, no one entering our order has made that choice for years. Mother Superior has decided that we should bring our few cloistered sisters back into the world. We plan to put their secular abilities to use—Sister Ursula, we knew, had been composing hymns for years—so we brought her here to lecture to you girls on music." Sister Olga picked up a pencil from her desk and began to roll it absently between her fingers. "You *are* learning about music, aren't you?"

"Oh, yes, Sister," I said quickly.

"Sister Ursula has not seen a newspaper or magazine since she took her vows—she's not uninformed about history, of course—the wars, the presidents, the new Pope, that sort of thing—but she only knows what she's been told. And since no one ever guessed that she was interested in Nijinsky—" Sister Olga coughed discreetly. "We've just told her. She seemed to take it calmly. We showed her the article in the encyclopedia."

I leaned back in my chair, beginning to feel relaxed. "Was she a dancer? Did she used to live in Paris?"

Sister Olga shrugged. "We know nothing about her except what she herself tells us. There weren't any files kept on girls who entered the convent before the First World War. We don't even know her exact age—she seems to have forgotten. Now as for the other part of your complaint—" Sister Olga laughed. "When I was a girl we were warned about patent leather shoes."

"My mother told me about that," I said.

"Sister Ursula has very old-fashioned notions about decency." Sister Olga stood up, her rosary clicking. "But you get the Church's modern view in your Family and Marriage class, don't you."

I nodded vigorously.

"Just relax and be a little understanding. Sister Ursula doesn't have advanced views about the behavior of young women—but you shouldn't let her upset you." Sister Olga moved across to the door, and stood holding the knob.

I rose to go. "Thank you, Sister. I feel much better."

"Good. I'm glad to get those cobwebs out of your head. I'd rather you didn't gossip about poor Sister Ursula, however— we're trying to make her adjustment to the modern world as easy as possible."

"I won't say a word to anyone," I promised.

Sister Olga opened the door for me. I heard the clatter of the typewriter as I passed the secretary's desk, but I was suddenly so light-headed and buoyant that I could hardly see ahead of me. The bell rang for the change of classes. I was caught up in the stream of brown-uniformed girls moving down the main hallway.

* * * * *

The Little Theater was empty on Friday when we filed in for our music lecture. Andrea found a seat beside me. She blew her nose into a pink tissue, then rolled the tissue into a ball. "Are you scared?" she asked.

"Not any more."

"Good." She stuffed her tissue into her torn jacket pocket. "She's just a crazy old nun."

"I don't think she's crazy," I said carefully. "She's just old. I feel sorry for her."

The side door near the stage opened, and Sister Ursula entered. We all quieted and coughed and cleared our throats. The movie screen had been rolled down, and Sister Ursula's headdress made a fantastic shadow against the white as she passed in front of it.

She stopped at the podium. She stretched out her arms and gripped it tightly. Her face once again seemed fuzzy to me—I decided that the eerie paleness of her skin was due to her many years in the cloister.

"She doesn't have any eyebrows," Andrea whispered.

"They're white. You just can't see them," I whispered back.

"Girls," Sister Ursula said sharply, "I have an apology to make to one of you." She turned her head slowly from side to side. "Where is the girl who told me that Nijinsky was dead?"

We looked around at each other. Finally someone said, "She's not here today, Sister."

Sister Ursula bowed her head. Her chin seemed to fold into the stiff cloth of her wimple. When she looked up again, she was squinting. The skin beneath her eyes appeared swollen.

"Then let me," she said, her voice cracking, "apologize to the rest of you instead. That girl was right. Nijinsky is dead. Nijinsky is dead," she repeated. "It's written down, so it must be true." She paused and looked blankly around as if she did not know where she was. "And he was mad—all those years he was mad."

I saw the curly head of the girl in the row ahead of me nodding in agreement.

"Let me tell you something," Sister Ursula went on, her voice stronger than before but still hollow and directed more at herself than at us. "I never had a vocation."

Again she paused. She seemed to be shivering and I leaned forward nervously. I was afraid she might have a stroke. Sister Olga had said that she took the news of Nijinsky's death calmly, but she did not look calm now. Beside me, Andrea reached down for her Spanish book. Out of the corner of my eye I saw her surreptitiously open it on her lap.

"I didn't go into the convent because I wanted to serve God. I went into the convent because I thought I was going mad myself. You see, I was never happy, girls. Never! Never in my whole life—I was born with an iron band around my heart, I think. There are weights in the tips of my fingers."

Sister Ursula extended her arm in front of her, trying to spread out her fingers which curled inward toward her palm. I could not take my eyes away from her face. It no longer seemed fuzzy to me. I could see every line in her skin and below it the pulsations of her muscles.

She brought her arm slowly back to her side. "And what about the wings on my shoulders?" she asked. "Can you see them?"

I heard someone snickering behind me, but most of the girls whose faces I could see had their eyes rigidly downcast.

"Can any one of you see my black wings?" she asked again. "Of course not. That's why I went into the convent—to hide them under my habit. At night, when I'm sleeping, the wings close over my body. I have the most evil dreams about Nijinsky. I've tried to live a holy life, but it's no use—when I'm writing my hymns, the evil wings brush the paper—I write horrible things."

I found I was gripping the metal armrests until my fingers ached. I glanced desperately at Andrea, but she was hunched over her book, mouthing Spanish words to herself. No one in the whole room seemed to be looking directly at Sister Ursula. Every girl I saw when I turned my head was slumped down in her seat as far as possible, horrified or embarrassed. I was the only one up on the edge of my chair. I tried to shut my eyes, but they opened of their own accord. I fought hard against the idea that was growing in the back of my mind: I had more in common with Sister Ursula than with anyone else in my new school.

Sister Ursula groaned loudly. "What have I done? I've frightened all of you, haven't I? But I only meant to apologize, I only meant to make you understand—oh, I'm wretched, wretched!"

She buried her face in her hands.

Maura Stanton was born in Evanston, Illinois in 1946 and grew up in Peoria, Chicago, and Minneapolis. She received a Master of Fine Arts from the Iowa Writers' Workshop. She currently lives in Bloomington, Indiana, where she chairs the Creative Writing Program at Indiana State University and directs the Indiana University Writers' Conference.

She is the recipient of many national awards, including the Yale Series of Younger Poets Award for her first book of poetry, *Snow on Snow* (Yale University Press, 1975). *Cries of Swimmers* was published by Utah University Press in 1984, and a third book, *Tales of the Supernatural*, will be published by Godine in 1988. Stanton published a novel, *Molly Companion* (Bobbs Merrill, 1977; Avon paperbacks, 1979), which was set in South America, and reprinted in Spanish as *Rio Abajo*. Her poems and stories have appeared in many magazines, including *The New Yorker, Poetry, American Poetry Review, The Atlantic, Crazyhorse,* the *Michigan Quarterly Review*, and *Ploughshares*.